The corpse was almos
Death was curiously m
Mel Edmunds was red
error.

Hawker swayed. His ten   , his eyes filmed
over, nausea rose within him. He shook himself in a
supreme effort to impose control. Kneeling beside the
body, he felt pulse and heart for signs of life. There
were none.

Also by the same author:

STONE DEAD

MARTiN INiGO

TOUCH PLAY

SPHERE BOOKS LTD

A *SPHERE* Book

First published in Great Britain by Sphere Books Ltd, 1991

Photoset in North Wales by
Derek Doyle & Associates, Mold, Clwyd.
Printed in Great Britain by
BPCC Hazell Books
Aylesbury, Bucks, England
Member of BPCC Ltd.

ISBN 0 7474 0203 5

Sphere Books Ltd
A Division of
Macdonald & Co (Publishers) Ltd
Orbit House
1 New Fetter Lane
London EC4A 1AR
A member of Maxwell Macmillan Pergamon Publishing Corporation

To Barbara Boote,
a patient and perceptive editor

'Sportswriting? There's nothing to it. You merely sit at the typewriter and think until the blood seeps out of the pores on your forehead.'

Red Smith

Chapter One

Don Hawker shifted uneasily on his chair and glanced around with misgiving. Luxury always made him feel uncomfortable. It brought out his guilt and resentment. A grudging envy troubled him. He feared for his integrity.

Hawker was sitting at one of the long parallel tables on the terrace at the Monte Carlo Country Club. Gulls circled overhead. A light breeze came in off the sea. Warm sunshine threw dazzling patterns on to the crisp, freshly-laundered, salmon-pink tablecloths. An exquisite lunch had been exquisitely served. The wine was chilled to perfection.

Sleek, bronzed and beautiful, the Riviera women were a study in offhand sophistication, birds of paradise in designer sunglasses. The cool, clear air was charged with their fragrance. The men were older, fatter, more watchful. Even in shirt sleeves and slacks, they managed to look blatantly prosperous as they toyed with their food or sipped their glasses of Chablis.

There was a languid arrogance about the scene. Effortless wealth on display. Tax exiles in open conspiracy. The freemasonry of the very rich. Hawker felt a sharp twinge of poverty.

A ripple of applause shook him out of his reverie.

'*Egalité!*'

The umpire's voice took his attention back to the centre court down below. Like the other privileged

1

spectators on the terrace, he had come to the first semi-final at the Monte Carlo Open tennis tournament. Mel Edmunds was playing Guido Barelli. America versus Italy. It was a grudge match. Hawker knew why.

The contrast between the two of them was striking. Slim, lithe and athletic, Mel Edmunds was a supreme touch player, an instinctive genius whose quicksilver brilliance had won him the men's singles title at Wimbledon the previous June. A mop of fair hair was held in check by a white headband but nothing could restrain his exuberance. He buzzed with vitality. Constantly on the move, he talked non-stop to himself, congratulating, scolding or exhorting as the occasion demanded. Mel Edmunds lived for his tennis.

Guido Barelli was carved out of solid rock. Dark, muscular and daunting, he was a glowering giant with matted hair on his arms, legs and chest. A satanic handsomeness reinforced the impression of hirsute virility. He had a speed about the court which belied his bulk but the essence of his game remained his heavy serve and booming volley. On the circuit, he was known as 'Blitzkreig'. It was not an affectionate nickname.

Hawker watched with interest. As a rule, the American would have little difficulty in handling someone who was nine places below him in the rankings yet he was struggling to hold his serve in the opening game. Mel Edmunds was patently out of form and he chided himself aloud. Spurred on by something which put extra venom into his strokes, the Italian pressed home his advantage. He took the game with a fierce cross-court passing shot which left his opponent scything the air.

Prolonged applause greeted the break of serve.

'Jesus!'

Katie Britwell bit her lip in apprehension.

Her husband was suffering down there and she was suffering with him. Katie was totally involved. She played each shot with Mel, chased each screaming return and shared each stab of pain as a point was surrendered. It was going to be a gruelling game for Mrs Edmunds.

'Come on!' she urged through gritted teeth.

'Early days yet,' reminded Hawker.

'He can slaughter Barelli.'

'Give him time.'

'Mel *has* to win this one.'

The next game began and Katie was caught up in its swirling drama. Hawker looked across at his companion. She seemed so small, young and vulnerable. Twisting a serviette between nervous fingers, she let out a gasp of horror as her husband netted a forehand volley. She had eaten no food. A glass of Perrier stood untouched on the table. Other priorities beckoned.

Appraising her now, Hawker found it hard to believe that she was the bright hope of British tennis. Her shoulders were hunched, her body tense, her face whitewashed with concern. There was no hint of the indomitable spirit which had taken her near the top of the women's rankings. She was a different woman.

Katie Britwell was that rarity on the international circuit. A consistent British winner. Ignoring the fact that she had spent her formative years in America, the nation took her to its heart but that heart missed a beat when – suddenly and inexplicably – she married Mel Edmunds. Apart from anything else, she had been engaged to someone else at the time.

'Aw, shit!' she cried over the applause.

The second game had just fallen to Barelli.

'Get your act together, Mel!'

Her husband was telling himself the same thing, thumping his racket head into the palm of his hand, plainly disgusted with his performance. Instead of taking a respite at the change-over, he went straight to the baseline at the other end of the court. The audible self-analysis continued.

Katie allowed herself a sip of Perrier.

'Not again,' she murmured. '*Please.*'

Hawker understood. Mel Edmunds was going through a nightmare period. In the previous season, he carried all before him and fought his way to the verge of a Grand Slam. After winning the Australian Open, the French Open and Wimbledon, he was only narrowly beaten in the final of the US Open, and there were several other tournament victories as well. Then came the wedding.

Since that, he had won absolutely nothing.

Barelli was determined that the losing sequence should go on. He came out for the third game with a scowl of concentration. The American served and underwent another bombardment.

Hawker's attention shifted to the front row seats directly behind the umpire's chair. Lia Barelli had chosen her position with as much care as her stunning red dress. The tall, elegant beauty who had graced the covers of all the leading fashion magazines wanted to be close to her husband to cheer him on. She also hoped to distract his opponent. Mel Edmunds was playing both of them.

Beside Lia was the massive frame of Vincente, an ex-wrestler who worked as the Barelli bodyguard. Bald, battle-scarred and expressionless, Vincente was good at his job. If his employer won the match and was mobbed by his many female fans, the bodyguard would earn his money. He liked that kind of action.

Katie was twisting her serviette again. Her body was tense and her teeth gritted. Lia Barelli, on the other hand, smiled serenely. It was as if the game were being played solely for her benefit. Two supreme athletes vying for her favour. A fight to the death in the sunshine. It gave her a sense of power, especially as her champion was in the ascendant. She and Vincente applauded as Barelli went even further ahead.

Hawker did not look at the court. He read the entire match in the faces of the two wives. When the Italian surged away to take the first set, Lia wore an expression of calm triumph, Katie was shattered. When Mel Edmunds somehow clung on to win a tie-break at the end of the second, Katie rallied enough to put her serviette aside and Lia glared her disapproval. Throughout the long and uncompromising third set, both women shuttled between delight and despair as the advantage swung first one way and then the other.

Class finally told. The American produced some magical shots to achieve a service break that gave him game, set and match. Mel Edmunds raised both arms aloft as he savoured his victory. He blew a kiss to his wife then glanced across involuntarily at Lia. Her eyes flashed and she rose angrily from her seat to make her way along the row.

Guido Barelli did not wait for the traditional handshake. Ignoring his opponent altogether, he gathered up his rackets and stalked off court. It had been much more than a game of tennis to him. He had wanted revenge and would now have to get it another way. Vincente looked as if he might have some ideas on the subject.

Katie clapped wildly and danced on her toes. Her husband had reached his first final in six months. The nightmare was almost over. Mel Edmunds was on the come-back trail.

A wave of deep sadness washed over Hawker. Without knowing why, he felt immensely sorry for Katie Britwell. She had come through an ordeal to find a joyful release. Hawker was pleased about that. In her moment of celebration, however, he sensed that tragedy lay ahead. It made him want to reach out to protect her.

The house was magnificent. Perched on a cliff that overlooked the bay, it was an elegant, neo-classical masterpiece in white marble. Large rooms were stocked with tasteful furniture that was complemented by superb oil paintings and striking *objets d'art*. Intricately woven Persian rugs were set off by the gleaming floors. Startling flower arrangements erupted from ornate vases at every turn and filled the whole house with their heady scent. Huge mirrors increased the abiding sense of space and colour.

There was nothing random about the place. Everything had been chosen with care and positioned with skill. Ordered luxury reigned. Nance Paulson looked completely at home in her surroundings. The daughter of a wealthy Boston financier, she was used to this kind of exaggerated comfort. Nance was a tall, slim woman with the loose-limbed grace of a natural athlete. Her face was interesting rather than attractive but it needed no make-up. Short, dark hair was brushed back severely from a high forehead. In a flowing white silk dress with a jewelled brooch on one shoulder, she was an arresting sight.

Nance raised her glass with a playful smile.

'To us!' she announced.

'To us!' echoed Jean-Louis.

'Yes,' murmured Dimitri.

'To us!' agreed Alain, tossing his mane. 'And especially to *me*, darlings. At my age, I need all the help I can get.'

They sipped their drinks. Nance had freshly-squeezed orange juice while the men preferred vintage champagne. It was evening and they were relaxing in cane chairs in the living room. The warmth of the afternoon had given way to a refreshing coolness.

Nance Paulson enjoyed her occasional role as a hostess. It made a welcome change from jetting around the world to play tennis. She was surprised how important the Monte Carlo home had become.

Nance never regretted her decision to marry a leading French businessman who was twenty years older than herself. Jean-Louis Croizier had much to recommend him. Calm, assured and devoted, he was responsive to her every wish and whim. Instead of hindering her tennis career, he had helped it to blossom even more. The thinning hair and the pencil moustache might be flecked with grey, but he was still a very handsome man. When he wore a white tuxedo, like tonight, he cut a real dash.

Jean-Louis beamed at his guests and raised a quizzical eyebrow.

'What did you think of the match?' he asked.

'Oh, we *loved* it, didn't we, Dimitri?' prompted Alain.

'Yes,' said his companion politely.

'All that masculine vitality. All that naked blood lust. It was positively delicious!' Alain Dupont sighed with pleasure. 'I felt like a Roman emperor watching two gladiators and I can take any amount of that kind of action. Highly stimulating.'

'Mel Edmunds was lucky to win,' noted Jean-Louis.

'He's twice the player Barelli is,' argued Nance.

'He did not look it today, *ma chère*.'

'Give the guy a break, will you?' she said easily. 'He's been having a tough time. Happens to us all sooner or later. One thing's for sure, though, Mel Edmunds has got more talent in his little finger than Barelli has in his whole anatomy.'

'From what I hear,' observed Alain wickedly, 'his talent is not confined to his little finger.'

Jean-Louis shrugged an explanation. 'Lia Barelli is a most beautiful woman.'

'It was only a rumour,' said Nance dismissively.

7

'I can believe it,' admitted her husband.

'So can I,' supported Alain. 'More to the point, the glowering Guido obviously believes it as well. I know he likes to play the field himself but those roving husbands are always the worst. Hideously jealous when their own wives are concerned. Beats me why men like that bother to get married at all. But then marriage itself has always been an enigma to me.'

Alain Dupont drank some more champagne and purred quietly. He was a small, wiry, wizened man in his seventies with long silver hair that fell to his shoulders and a leathery face that was contoured by years of systematic dissipation. Alain was a distinguished artist who specialized in portraits of sporting and showbiz celebrities. He had lived on the Riviera for almost half a century and was one of its most enduring and out-rageous characters.

Dimitri was a slender Greek in his twenties with classic good looks. Alain always had someone like Dimitri in tow. He himself might grow older but the age of his friends remained fairly constant. Wearing a pale blue suit of the finest cotton, Dimitri was silent and watchful. Evidently, he was a recent acquisition and still somewhat in awe of his flamboyant partner. Alain himself sported an open-necked red shirt beneath a baggy suit of black satin. Red canvas shoes completed the outfit.

Despite his name, Alain Dupont was an Englishman in exile. One of his many affectations was to speak with a light Yorkshire accent. In every other respect, his emigration from Doncaster was comprehensive.

He turned solicitous blue eyes upon his hostess.

'I forgot to ask about your elbow.'

'Much better, thanks,' she said.

'An occupational hazard.'

'I've learned to live with it.'

'Will you be able to play in the Italian Open?'

'Try stopping me, Alain.'

'I wouldn't *dare*!'

'Oh, I hate having to pull out of a tournament,' she continued with a sigh, 'but it has its compensations. Instead of being over in Houston right now, I'm able to have fun with friends.'

'What about Katie Britwell?' pressed Alain. 'She's fully fit, isn't she? Why did she opt out of the Virginia Slims this week?'

'Why else?' asked Jean-Louis. 'To be with her husband.'

'That's right,' confirmed Nance. 'Mel's had such a terrible run lately, she felt she had to be here to hold his hand.'

'Seems to have worked,' noted the artist.

She nodded. 'So far.'

'It just goes to prove the value of marriage,' said Jean-Louis with a lazy grin. 'Wives can come in useful sometimes.'

'We'll have to take your word for it,' decided Alain. 'Won't we, Dimitri?'

The Greek displayed a perfect set of teeth.

A doorbell rang in the distance and Nance got to her feet at once. The other guests had arrived and she was anxious to be the first to greet them. After a few moments, the door opened and a maidservant ushered in Mel Edmunds and Katie Britwell.

'Come on in!' welcomed Nance.

'Hi, everyone!' they said in unison.

She embraced them both with brisk affection. Jean-Louis came over to kiss Katie on the cheeks and to pump Mel's hand. Nance then introduced the newcomers to Alain and Dimitri. When drinks had been poured – orange juice for Katie, Perrier for Mel – they all sat down. The new arrivals were side by side on a cane settee. They were casually dressed and in good spirits. Mel's victory that afternoon had cheered both of them.

'Congratulations!' began Jean-Louis.

'Thanks,' said Mel.

'You played some great shots today,' complimented Alain.

'I was lousy and I know it.'

'You still won,' reminded Katie, squeezing his hand.

'I'll play better tomorrow.'

'You'll have to, darling,' said Alain knowledgeably. 'Yuri Chegenyov will give you a much harder battle than Barelli. The Ruskie is at his best on clay. He crucified Holmgren in his semi-final. I know you beat Chegenyov at Wimbledon but it took you five sets and he stretched you all the way. Nobody can slice a ball as well as he can and that backhand of his is lethal.'

'Who are you?' asked Mel, bridling. 'His press agent?'

'A well-wisher.'

'Yeah?'

'An interested observer, dear heart.'

'I'm *not* your dear heart.'

'The night is young,' teased Alain.

'Back off, man.'

Jean-Louis stepped in smartly to defuse the sudden tension.

'It really is wonderful to see Mel and Katie here at last. We thought that it would never happen. All four of us in Monte Carlo at the same time. *C'est impossible!*'

'Complete fluke,' agreed Nance.

'Fabulous house!' admired Katie, looking around.

'We like it, too,' said Jean-Louis warmly. 'Nance will give you both a tour later on. We bought it as our little hideaway. Everyone needs a place where they can just lock out the rest of the world.'

'Sure thing,' said Katie.

'So when are you two going to buy a house?' asked Nance.

The young couple exchanged an uneasy glance.

Mel shrugged. 'The apartment is okay for the time being.'

'And where might it be?' wondered Alain.

'New York.'

'Dreadful place!' opined the artist with a shudder.

'It suits us,' said Mel firmly. 'New York is where it all happens. Live in a city like that and everywhere else seems so goddam provincial. I like to be at the centre of events.'

'But we'll have a house one day, sweetie,' insisted Katie.

'Yeah – in Manhattan.'

'Don't write off Monaco,' urged Jean-Louis. 'I know they say that it is not what it used to be but it is still very special. Tell them, Alain. You have been here longer than any of us. You are the expert, *mon ami*.'

'Yes,' sighed Alain, taking his cue. 'I first came to the Riviera when it *was* the Riviera. Civilized yet supremely scandalous. It was sublime! And classy. None of this modern riff-raff.' He winked at Dimitri. 'Of course, I was even younger than you then. A wide-eyed lad from dear old Doncaster with a burning ambition to paint. Do you know what my name was? Alf Bridge. It's true. Alfred Bridge. *Very* artistic! Can you imagine signing that at the bottom of a masterpiece? It took me just three days to change it to Alain Dupont. That's what the Riviera did for me. Gave me a whole new identity.'

Before he could continue the story, there was a tap on the door and the pretty young maidservant entered.

'*Excusez-moi*,' she said. '*Telefon. Mademoiselle Britwell.*'

'For me?' Katie was surprised.

'Take it in the hall,' suggested Nance.

'Oh, right . . .'

'Show her the way, Valerie.'

'*Oui, Madame.*'

Katie followed her out and closed the door as she went. Alain needed no encouragement to take up where he had left off. His memoirs of the Riviera were

11

at once engaging and shocking but they were also highly amusing and all but Mel were soon chuckling happily. It was only when Alain finished that Nance realized how long Katie had been away on the telephone.

'I'll go see what's keeping her,' she volunteered.

As his wife slipped out, Jean-Louis crossed to the little bar to replenish the drinks. He was an affable host who liked his guests to have a good time at his home. He chatted about a racing yacht that he was thinking of buying. Mel Edmunds showed some interest at last. Sailing was one of his few hobbies.

Nance, meanwhile, stood in the hall and watched Katie. The latter was so absorbed in her conversation that she did not even notice the other woman. Whoever had rung Katie had given her bad news. Her face was puckered and her voice was breathless with agitation.

'I just can't . . . not tomorrow . . .'

She winced as something was said to her down the line.

'That's not fair . . . *Please*! . . . Listen to me . . .'

But the caller had rung off. Stunned and hurt, Katie stared at the receiver for a full minute before she replaced it. She took a deep breath and brought a hand up to her forehead. Nance stepped towards her.

'Everything okay, honey?'

'Oh!' Katie almost jumped.

'Sorry to scare you.'

'Didn't realize you were there.'

'Who was that?'

'It was . . . personal.'

'Trouble?'

'No, no,' said Katie hurriedly. 'Nothing like that.'

'And you feel okay?' Nance asked softly.

'Fine, fine. Let's go back and join the party . . .'

Katie swished off towards the living room and led

the way in. Mel was talking about his sailing days. He broke off as his wife sat down beside him and reached for her drink.

'Who was it?' he said.

'Daddy.'

'Calling you *here*?'

'The hotel knew where to find me.'

'What did the old guy want?'

'Tell you later, Mel.' She gulped down her orange juice then offered an apologetic smile to the others. 'Sorry about that.'

'No problem,' assured Jean-Louis, striding across to the bar again. 'You are just in time for the highlight of the evening, Katie. Now, *mes amis*, you may think you came here just to dine with us but there is more to it than that. *Eh, ma chère?*' He reached behind the bar counter and brought out a large, oblong painting that was covered in a white sheet. '*Mon Dieu!* What do we have here?'

Jean-Louis propped the painting up against the table so that they could all see it. Dimitri was intrigued, Mel was puzzled, Katie was still preoccupied. The others all knew what was going on. Jean-Louis took hold of the bottom corner of the sheet.

'*Mesdames et messieurs*, it is my pleasure to unveil the latest and greatest work by Alain Dupont.' He whisked away the sheet with a flourish. '*Regardez! C'est magnifique, non?*'

The portrait of Nance Paulson was arresting. She was about to serve in a match during the US Open at Flushing Meadow. Her racket was inches away from contact with the ball. Teeth were bared, eyes were narrowed, arm was at full stretch, muscles were tensed, sinews were strained and every ounce of her being was concentrated on the job in hand. Power, grace and determination were blended into a perfect whole and the painting had captured it with the accuracy of a

13

camera. Dimitri clapped in approval, Katie was trans-
fixed and even Mel was impressed. For all his idiosyn-
crasies, Alain Dupont had a unique talent for sporting
portraiture.

'Definitive Alf Bridge!' he commented.

'Wonderful!' said Dimitri.

'Say, that's pretty good,' conceded Mel.

'Fantastic!' added Katie. 'I mean . . . it's amazing.'

Alain lay back in his chair and basked in the
admiration.

'From Suzanne Lenglen to Nance Paulson,' he said.
'I've painted all the stars of women's tennis. And the
men, of course. Starting with Big Bill Tilden himself –
and what a dear, sweet human being he was!'

'You have a gift, Alain,' said Jean-Louis.

'It's magic,' whispered Dimitri.

'Quite superb,' endorsed Katie.

'Glad you think so,' said Nance, 'because you have a
chance to put your money where your mouth is. Alain is
in great demand but he will consider it as a favour to us.'

'Consider what?' asked Mel.

'Let him in on the secret,' suggested Nance.

'Secret?'

'Yes,' said Katie. 'Part of the reason for coming
here this evening was to meet Alain. I've heard so much
about him and loved everything of his that I've seen.
Particularly, this new one.'

'So?' said Mel.

'I want him to do a portrait of you.'

'*Me*?' There was a note of hostility.

'It would be a pleasure to work with you,' said Alain
gently.

'I'd be commissioning it,' said Katie eagerly. 'It would
be a present from me to you. What do you think, Mel?'

'No,' he retorted.

'Don't reject the idea out of hand.'

'Alain is the best in the business,' urged Nance.

14

'At *what*, though?'

'Mel!' chided his wife.

'You insult a close friend of mine,' warned Jean-Louis. 'It is an honour to be the subject of a painting by Alain Dupont.'

'Then it's one I'll have to miss out on,' said Mel.

'We haven't even discussed it,' complained Katie.

'No discussion needed.'

'But I *want* a portrait of you.'

'Too bad!'

'What have you got against the idea?'

'Two main things,' he countered. 'First, I hate the feeling of being set up. Of being the victim of someone else's plans.'

'And second?' asked Nance.

'Nothing personal,' he continued, 'but I don't want that guy anywhere near me.'

'You'd only have to sit a few times,' said Alain casually. 'I work largely from photographs.'

'I can guess what kind!' said Mel.

'Take care, *M'sieur*!' shouted Jean-Louis angrily.

'That was uncalled-for,' said Nance.

'Mel didn't mean it,' bleated Katie.

'I can speak for myself,' he said.

'We can see that,' mocked Alain.

'Then get out of my face,' said the American. 'You're in such demand, go do portraits of someone else. Last thing I need in my life right now is a fag painter!'

During the long, awkward silence that followed, Katie Britwell was puce with embarrassment. Nance was disgusted, Jean-Louis was livid and Alain himself was deeply offended even though he did not show it. But it was Dimitri who had the most profound reaction. Smarting on his friend's behalf, he glared at the culprit with frightening intensity. Fury smouldered within him.

Mel Edmunds knew how to antagonize.

Taking care not to wake her, Don Hawker slipped out of bed and crept across to the washbasin. Even though it was cool in the room, his naked body was glistening with sweat. He ran cold water to bathe his face then dried himself all over. When he put on his shorts, vest and running shoes, he let himself out as quietly as he could. He came out of the hotel to find the principality blanketed by dark cloud. The stiff breeze was a tonic as it plucked at his hefty frame.

Hawker ran in the direction of the sea. His action was low, unhurried and economical. He leaned forward from the waist, his elbows protruded comically as his arms swung to and fro across his chest, and his craggy face had the look of a martyr in search of new suffering. For a distance runner, he seemed altogether too solid and muscular yet he covered the ground without apparent effort at a pace that was dictated by some inner stopwatch. Hawker had never been the most elegant of British athletes but few had been more successful or more controversial. Even though his track career was now decisively over, he could not stop running. It was a compulsion.

It was still not six and the streets were mercifully deserted. Tree-lined boulevards which would later turn into glorified traffic jams were now seductive ribbons of emptiness. Narrow lanes which would later be clogged with jostling humans still enjoyed their nocturnal freedom. No rubbish spilled out of the litter bins or blew about in the gutters. No graffiti defaced the walls. The fairy-tale state of Monaco was the cleanest spot on the Riviera. Money was its refuse. Its howling slogans were confined to advertising hoardings.

Hawker ran a quarter of a mile before he saw his first milk lorry and he reached Boulevard du Bord de

16

la Mer before he met a paper van. With the sea on his right, he settled into an easy rhythm and pounded along towards the Old Town. High-rise apartments and luxury hotels stretched out on his left with a scattering of expensive shops and restaurants. It was a hostile environment for someone like Hawker. He blocked out his surroundings and thought about the day ahead.

Katie Britwell moved to the forefront of his mind. She was more than a friend. She touched off all sorts of generous responses inside him and he could not understand why. He admired her as a player and as a person yet he feared for her. Was it because she was married to Mel Edmunds? Was it because she was caught up in the savage world of professional tennis? Or did it have something to do with her resemblance to Elaine? Not that there was any physical similarity between them. It was their manner. That faintly unguarded attitude to life. Hawker had plenty to occupy him as he ran around the perimeter of the Old Town. It made him oblivious to all else.

When he finally got back to his modest little hotel, it was well past seven. He went up to his room, let himself in and reached for his towel. A hand emerged from the bedclothes to wave to him. A blonde head soon followed. Bleary eyes tried to focus.

'Where have you been?' she said.

'Running.'

'*Again?*'

'I like it.'

'More than me?'

Hawker grinned. 'Lots more.'

'Bastard!'

Christina Erikkson sat up in bed and shook herself fully awake. Pouting with mock annoyance, she wagged a finger at him. Her English was good but overlaid with a heavy Swedish accent.

'You do not deserve me. You know that?'

17

'Calm down.'

'When I spend a night with a man, I expect – how do you say it in English – I expect my money's worth!'

'You mean, I get *paid*?' he teased.

'I wanted you here!' she insisted, thumping the pillow.

'But you were fast asleep.'

'Makes no difference.'

'Christina, I needed my run.'

'I should come first.'

'No comment.'

He tried to appease her with a smile then turned to the door.

'Where are you going *now*?' she demanded.

'To take a shower.'

'Hawker, you are . . . impossible.'

'I'm all lathered up,' he reasoned.

'If only we'd stayed at *my* hotel,' she argued. 'We could have had our own private bathroom. But – no! You make me stay here instead.'

'I'm old-fashioned, that's why.'

'But I had the better room.'

'Agreed. But I didn't pay for it.'

'Who cares?'

'I do.'

'Why?'

'Call it male ego, if you like.'

'I know what I call it,' she snapped. 'I think you have no consideration for me at all.'

Another grin. 'Dead right.'

Christina hurled the pillow at him but he was much too fast. It spent its venom on the door as it closed behind him, then fell harmlessly to the floor. Hawker went happily along the corridor to the bathroom and stripped off. Christina Erikkson was a delight. She had helped to make his trip bearable. As he stepped under the shower and let the warm water cascade all over

18

him, he thought about the way she had singled him out, chatted him up and more or less propositioned him. A sports photographer for a leading Swedish newspaper, Christina was a bright, attractive, high-stepping young lady with a mind of her own.

Hawker realized why he liked her so much.

She did not remind him in any way of Elaine.

By the time the final of the Monte Carlo Open was due to be played, the wind had died down and the clouds had drifted away. Muted sunlight looked down on stands that were splashed with colour and keyed up with expectation. The spectators were being offered a rerun of the Wimbledon final. Mel Edmunds against Uri Chegenyov. Every cliché about East and West had been pressed into service, and all kinds of spurious political significance was read into the encounter. The Russian player was the firm favourite because of his expertise on clay.

Hawker arrived early so that he could drink in the atmosphere and made a full appraisal of the event. He was glad that he would not be sitting with the rest of the press corps, who viewed him with a suspicion that shaded into outright antagonism in some cases. They were the established tennis writers and he was the usurper. Much to their chagrin, he had achieved what they had all signally failed to get – a series of exclusive interviews with Mel Edmunds and Katie Britwell. Since their marriage, the couple had kept the press steadfastly at bay and refused to divulge anything about their private life. Don Hawker now had privileged access to them. The sports magazine for which he wrote was delighted. Their man had a knack of pipping everyone else to the post.

When he looked around the stadium, therefore, Hawker was not surprised to collect some hard stares. It was not just his scoop that was resented. There was the small matter of Christina Erikkson who had been targeted by more than one scribe. Yet Hawker had snaffled her up from under the noses of these other self-appointed suitors. It did not increase his popularity.

He gazed up at the terrace of the Country Club in time to see Nance Paulson arriving with her husband. As the world's number one woman player, she caused a mild stir among the people around her and many heads turned to stare up from the stands. The couple were soon joined by Alain Dupont and the attentive Dimitri, the former in white suit and Panama hat, the latter in tight jeans, blue silk shirt and wrap-around sun-glasses.

More ripples of interest were shown when Guido and Lia Barelli appeared, ostentatiously holding hands and making much of each other. Hawker noted that Vincente was standing by one of the entrances and keeping his employer under surveillance. After a career of inflicting and withstanding pain, his huge body was still in prime condition. Like the Barellis, he had not come to enjoy the tennis for its own sake. He was there to see Mel Edmunds ground into submission. Nothing less would satisfy him.

As the last of the crowds streamed in, Hawker moved to take up his own seat. Christina came over to snatch a word with him. Cameras dangling from her neck, she was ready for action.

'Will I see you afterwards?' she wondered.

'Hope so.'

'Good. Come and find me.'

'Right,' he agreed. 'By the way, who's going to win?'

'Chegenyov,' she said confidently.

'Are you sure?'

'Yes. Uri gives me the best photos.'

She kissed him lightly on the cheek then went off to take up her position at the far end of the court with the

20

other photographers. Hawker went to his seat which was in the stand opposite the umpire. He had a perfect view and was rather puzzled that Katie Britwell did not turn up to share it with him. When the officials came out on court, the seat beside him remained vacant. He decided that Katie must be around the back somewhere with her husband, giving him some last-minute advice and encouragement, but this notion was quickly dispelled when the players appeared. Deaf to the applause that greeted his arrival, Mel Edmunds was plainly disconcerted when he looked across at the empty seat. At the time she was needed most, Katie was not there.

As the players began their knock-up, Hawker had the opportunity to study the Russian and he saw what Christina meant. Yuri Chegenyov was nothing if not photogenic. A compact figure of medium height, he had the face of a ballet dancer, at once strong and sensitive. His long black hair shone in the sun and lashed his cheeks whenever he turned his head sharply. He was a crowd favourite and knew how to use his expressive features to amuse and entertain.

Mel Edmunds, however, was in a mean mood and made no concession to the presence of spectators. Prancing nervously on his toes, he played his practice shots and talked aloud to himself. Like the Russian, he wore his sponsor's logo on his shirt, shorts, socks, shoes and racket. It was a battle of rival manufacturers.

When the allotted time was up, there was still no sign of Katie. Her husband took one last look at her seat then tried to oust her completely from his mind. Having won the toss and earned the right to serve, he took up his place on the baseline. The umpire set the game in motion and Mel Edmunds went through his usual ritual, bouncing the ball four times with his left hand before throwing it high and meeting it with a vicious smash.

It was a clean ace. Chegenyov did not get near it. He adjusted his position to receive the next serve but could only direct the ball into the net. His next return met the same fate. Emboldened by this early success, the American went for another ace but he was well out. A deep second serve, however, had the Russian scrambling and Mel was able to come to the net to dispatch a lame return with a crisp volley.

First blood to America. It would never be that easy again. Chegenyov soon showed why he was ranked only two places below his opponent. A penetrating serve forced Mel backwards then he raced to and fro across the baseline as the ball was hit to alternating corners. It was a long, punishing rally but Chegenyov was always in control, using subtle variations of pace, length, spin, angle and trajectory to keep his opponent on the defensive. He took the point with a shot that had become his hallmark – a sliced backhand down the line of quite astonishing speed and precision. The next three points also went to the Russian after gruelling rallies.

Chegenyov's tactics were clear. Younger and fitter, he was opting for a baseline game that would extend the rallies and sap Mel's stamina. When the Russian came out to gain a break of serve, it seemed as if his plan was working. Frustration soon set in and Mel began to come to the net to attack. Every time he did so, however, he was expertly lobbed and stranded in no man's land. He got some token points in each game but Chegenyov was romping away with the set.

As the Russian's lead increased, his manner became more arrogant. The crowd acclaimed the series of winners that he was hitting but Hawker was more interested in his behaviour at the change-over. Whenever the players got close to each other, he said something to his opponent which patently needled him. It was almost as if he was gloating and for Mel

Edmunds – nominally, the top player in the world – this was an unbearable insult.

But he could do nothing about it. Unable to translate anger into points, Mel lost the first set 6-1. He towelled off the perspiration and looked balefully in the direction of the empty seat. No Katie. No help from that quarter. He was on his own. After a long, reflective drink, he dried the handle of his racket and came out for the next set. There was an element of sympathy in the applause for him whereas his opponent got something bordering on an ovation.

Mel Edmunds brought greater patience and application to his game but still found himself trailing 3-0 in relatively short order. He was playing well yet losing badly. Chegenyov had the psychological advantage and the bulk of the spectators were behind him. Barelli and his wife were relishing every moment. Vincente was grinning broadly as if he had just broken someone's back. Up on the terrace, Nance Paulson and her party were not displeased with the situation either. Mel Edmunds had been at his most objectionable the previous evening. It was heartening to see him put in his place. Judging from the expression on Dimitri's face, however, it was not enough. He wanted more.

In the fourth game, everything changed. It began with the kind of brush with officialdom for which the American was notorious. He was 15-30 down when he served wide. Taking more time over his second serve, he hit it so deep and hard that Chegenyov could only guide it into the net. Simultaneously, a fault was called.

The umpire agreed with his linesman.

'*Quinze – quarante!*'

'You've got to be joking!' protested Mel.

'*Quinze – quarante!*'

'Aw, come on! That ball was good.'

'*Jouez, s'il vous plaît.*'

'Let's have some fairness around here, shall we!'

Mel quickly lost his temper and argument turned into abuse. Linesman and umpire thought the serve was out but Chegenyov had tried to return it. Mel appealed to him to confirm that the ball was in but the Russian would not be drawn into the dispute. Shrugging his shoulder he walked away and let the others fight it out. Mel's antics only upset the crowd and turned them vociferously against him. He was soon under fire from all sides. In the end, he had to accept the decision.

'*Quinze – quarante.*'

Sustained applause broke out and Mel was barracked in several languages. Chegenyov smiled. Hawker felt sorry for the American. With problems enough on his hands, the player now had everyone against him. He would surely crumble. Yet somehow he did not. The injustice of it all rankled and was put to good use. Adrenalin flowed. Defiance surged. Power returned. Mel served an ace to silence the rumbling antagonism. Moving to the other side of the court, he hit a high-kicking serve which made Chegenyov scoop the ball invitingly upwards. A fierce overhead smash took the score to deuce.

The game had been saved but not won. For nine more nail-biting minutes, they took it in turns to seize the advantage then squander it. Mel Edmunds finally settled the issue with a topspin forehand volley that sizzled past his opponent. He had not merely held serve. The whole course of the match had been altered.

It was an appropriate moment for Katie Britwell to arrive. Squeezing along the row, she sat down beside Hawker and looked up in dismay at the scoreboard.

'Jesus!' she exclaimed.

'Where've you been?'

'What's happening, Don?'

'Chegenyov's on song.'

'Mel can wipe the floor with him.'

'Not today.'

'He can't lose to Yuri!'

'Why weren't you here?'

'What? Oh, the flight was delayed in Paris.'

'*Paris?*'

'Forget about me,' she said evasively. 'It's Mel we have to worry about. He's taking a pasting out there. Against Yuri!'

'They don't exactly like each other, do they?'

'That's putting it mildly.'

'Personal or professional?'

'Both,' said Katie. 'Yuri's determined to get that number one spot whatever it costs – and not just for Mother Russia.'

'It would have tremendous propaganda value,' noted Hawker.

'He wants it for himself. Don't be fooled by all that smiling and playing to the crowd. Underneath, he's one ambitious son of a bitch. First time Mel ever took him on . . .'

Her voice tailed away as play resumed. Mel Edmunds did not need to glance across at her seat. He sensed that she was there and it put extra steel into his game. He had let Chegenyov take the initiative long enough. Now it was his turn to force the pace. He gave notice of his intent with a blistering return of serve that left his opponent flat-footed. The American was in top gear now, running tirelessly, fighting for every point as if his life depended on it, putting his full repertoire of shots on display.

Mel broke serve then held his own to level the score. Chegenyov came back to win the next game but it was his last. Playing wonderful, uninhibited tennis, Mel Edmunds took the second set with emphatic superiority. In the final set, miraculously, he somehow lifted his game to even greater heights. The Russian gave of his best but he was not equal to the free-flowing genius on the other side of the net. It was a superb exhibition of touch play and it reduced Chegenyov to a dispirited blob of sweat. As yet another cross-court passing shot left him gasping and concluded his ordeal, he hurled his racket to the ground in sheer desperation. Mel won the match 1-6, 6-4, 6-0.

The spectators showed their appreciation with prolonged applause. Mel Edmunds was the crowd favourite now. He had charmed them with his talents and come back from the dead to achieve a significant victory. The problems inherent in his game had at last been resolved. He acknowledged his ovation like a restored monarch. Guido Barelli, his wife and his bodyguard did not stop for the presentation ceremony. Nance Paulson and the others watched it with mixed feelings. Jean-Louis showed a grudging respect for Mel. Alain settled for an amused contempt. Dimitri was a study in suppressed anger. Only Nance, torn between admiration and disappointment, bothered to clap.

Katie Britwell was beside herself, shaking with excitement, shouting with joy and understanding more than anyone else the true implications of the result. Hawker was deeply impressed. When his back was to the wall, Mel had come out fighting and proved what an exceptional athlete he was. The journalist was thrilled for Katie, too, but his pleasure was tempered by apprehension.

Something was amiss. Hawker wished he knew what it was.

The hotel was a giant tube of glass, ferroconcrete and architectural ingenuity. Rising above all the buildings around it, the Hotel Brassard pointed up towards heaven like an altar candle. It had the finest facilities in Monaco and a cuisine which brought in gourmets from much further afield. Inevitably, it set a high price on its services and this acted as a useful filter. Only the rich visited the hotel. Only the very rich dared to stay there for any length of time.

Mel Edmunds liked to advertise his wealth. The young millionaire had taken a penthouse suite which commanded a sensational view of the maritime Alps. He felt that he worked hard on the tennis court. When he came off it, he liked to be pampered and that meant the premier hotel at every location on the tournament circuit. It was all part of the image that Mel liked to project.

Hawker was uneasy about coming to the Hotel Brassard. It was hardly his natural habitat. A fortnight's residence there would knock a substantial hole in his annual income. Even though he had been there before, he still entered the place as if half-expecting to be thrown out as a vagrant.

He was loping across the lobby when he was waylaid.

'Bless my soul – here *is* the fellow!'

'Oh, hello.'

'I was just taking your name in vain.'

'Were you?'

'With some of the chaps. In the bar.'

Quentin Rivers looked more like a retired colonel than the tennis correspondent of a national daily. Spruce, straight-backed and close to sixty, he had a round, florid face that converged on a natty grey moustache. His bald head had a military gleam to it and his voice had a jocular resentment.

'What's your secret, Hawker?'

'Secret?'

'What've *you* got that we haven't? Eh?' Rivers jabbed the stem of his pipe at him. 'I've been writing about tennis for over thirty years and I can't get close to the happy couple. You've been involved with the game for five minutes yet land an exclusive. How? That's what I'd like to know.'

'Charm,' said Hawker provocatively.

'Well, it doesn't bloody well work on me!'

'You'll have to excuse me . . .'

'Try the salon.'

'What?'

'The lovely Katie,' explained the other, thrusting his pipe back into his mouth. 'That's where you'll find her. Having her hair done. For your benefit, I daresay. After all, it's something of an honour to be interviewed by the great Don Hawker.'

The sarcasm washed harmlessly off its target. Hawker was all too accustomed to it by now. As he appraised Quentin Rivers, he caught a whiff of gin mingling with the tobacco smoke. He nodded a farewell but the older man detained him a little longer.

'Make the most of it while you can,' he advised.

'Eh?'

'The dynamic duo. Enjoy it while it lasts.'

'What are you on about?' asked Hawker.

'Their marriage. It's not a thing of beauty and a joy forever. You may have the inside track at the moment but it won't stay that way. When they split up – bang goes your story!'

'Who says they'll split up?'

'I do!' asserted Rivers with a sly grin. 'Put money on it. Mel Edmunds won't be tied down for much longer. He'll soon start pouncing on anything that moves. Poor Katie!' He thrust his face closer. 'I give it three months.'

'Three months?'

'Maximum.'

Quentin Rivers swung on his heel and headed for the exit, leaving Hawker to digest what had been said. It did not sit easily on his stomach. He dismissed the subject from his mind and went in search of the hairdressing salon. Mel and Katie were going to have a celebratory meal that evening in their suite and

28

Hawker had been invited to join them. He was looking forward to it. During the championship itself, they had both been tense and uncommunicative. He hoped that they would now be more relaxed and forthcoming.

The salon was a palatial lounge at the end of a corridor. Katie Britwell was its only customer. Seated in a chair, she was being fussed over by two young female assistants. Hawker took a few self-conscious steps into the room and cleared his throat. Katie caught sight of him in her mirror. She smiled a welcome.

'Don!'

'I was told I might find you here.'

'I wanted to be at my best,' she said. 'Very special occasion. Mel's first win since we got married.'

'Would you . . . like me to wait outside?'

'No, no. I'll be a little while yet. Go on up.'

'Is Mel there?'

'Yes.' She had second thoughts. 'Wait a minute! Maybe not.'

'I'll hang on for you, then.'

'It's okay. Mel might be in the bath, that's all. Here.' She leaned forward and took something from the table in front of her. 'Take this. If Mel doesn't answer the door, let yourself in.'

'Will that be okay?'

'Fine. He's expecting you.'

Katie leaned back in her chair and one of the assistants snipped away at her hair with a pair of small scissors. Hawker glanced down at the plastic card-key which had been handed to him.

'See you soon,' promised Katie.

'Right.'

Retracing his steps to the lobby, he went over to one of the lifts and pressed the call button. He got a response within seconds. Stepping into the empty lift, he inserted his card-key into the slot and the computer read the number of his room. The doors closed and he was whisked right up to the top of the building at controlled speed. Hawker came out into a corridor and searched for the room number that he wanted.

The more he got to know Katie Britwell, the more he liked her. By the same token, the more she reminded him of Elaine. It was quite unnerving. He tried to remember if Elaine had still been that much in love after six months of marriage. Would she have had her hair done for a special occasion like this? Had she been this devoted to her husband's career? The old pain returned. What did it matter?

He rehearsed some of the questions he was going to ask that evening. His magazine had been more than willing to send him to Monaco but they wanted results. Hawker had to get the story that no other journalist would write. Insight into a controversial marriage. Why did they choose each other? Did it work? What had it cost them? Would it last?

He found the room and pressed the doorbell. No answer.

'Mel! Mel, are you there?' he called.

He knocked hard on the timber with his knuckles.

'It's me. Don Hawker. Can you hear me, Mel?'

Still no reply. Evidently, his host was in the bath as Katie had predicted. He put the card-key into the slot and turned the silver knob. As he entered the room, the door closed silently behind him. Mel was nowhere to be seen. The bathroom door was wide open and the place was unoccupied. He looked across at the bedroom door.

'Mel!' he repeated. 'Katie told me to come on up.'

But there was no sound from the bedroom either. He started to walk across to it and then came to an abrupt halt. As he went past the massive sofa, he saw that Mel Edmunds was there after all. Wearing a white bathrobe, he was lying face down on the carpet with his body twisted at an awkward angle. The back of his skull had been smashed in and his head was islanded by a sea of blood that spread right across the thick pile.

Chapter Two

There was an air of unreality about the scene. The room was plush, spacious, colour-schemed. Fixtures and fittings were of the highest quality. Nothing had been skimped. The chandelier set the tone of glittering elegance. On a raised area in front of the double-glazed window, a table was set for three. Silver cutlery and cut-glass wine goblets gleamed above a damask tablecloth. A six-branched silver candelabra acted as a centrepiece. It was a dazzling room in every sense. Excess was only just held in check by good taste.

The corpse was almost smothered by its surroundings. Death was curiously minimized. Robbed of its drama. Mel Edmunds was reduced to some grotesque design error.

Hawker swayed. His temples pounded, his eyes filmed over, nausea rose within him. He shook himself and made a supreme effort to impose control. Kneeling beside the body, he felt pulse and heart for signs of life. There were none. Viewed close up, the head wound had an awesome finality to it. Only hours earlier, the player had been buzzing with energy on a tennis court. Every drop of that vitality had now been drained away for good.

Reaching for the telephone, Hawker dialled the number displayed on the instrument. The voice which came on the line was young, bright and female.

'*Allo! Reception . . .*'

'Can you speak English?' he asked.

'Of course, M'sieur. How can I help you, please?'

'Get me the manager.'

'What is the trouble, M'sieur?'

'I need to talk to the manager.'

'He is very busy. If you could tell me what —'

'This is an emergency!' he interrupted. 'Put me through!'

The urgency of his command had the desired affect.

There were some clicking sounds then a number rang out. Almost immediately, the receiver was snatched up and a deep voice was heard.

'*Allo!*'

'Is that the manager?' said Hawker.

'Yes, M'sieur.' Slight deference crept in. 'I am Henri Lequesne. Who is this, please?'

'My name is Hawker.'

'You are a guest at the hotel, M'sieur?'

'No,' he replied, trying not to gabble. 'I'm visiting some guests. In Room 1250. I think you should get up here as quickly as possible, Mr Lequesne. And send for the police.'

'The police!' repeated the other in alarm.

'We have a problem up here.'

'What kind of problem, M'sieur?'

'A dead body.'

After a stunned silence, a hoarse whisper came on the line.

'What room did you say, M'sieur?'

'1250. Mr and Mrs Edmunds.'

Putting down the receiver, Hawker took a few paces back to survey the scene. Familiarity did not lessen its impact on him. His stomach heaved afresh. Mel Edmunds was a sorry figure, hunched and motionless, lying in a crumpled heap near the marble-topped coffee table. Mingling with the blood was the white wine from an overturned glass that lay beside the body.

Between the glass and the shattered skull was a large, solid onyx ashtray, covered in blood and standing on its edge. Hawker wondered if it was the murder weapon or an incidental casualty of Mel's apparent fall against the coffee table.

He circled the corpse to view it from different angles, trying to work out the positions in which victim and attacker must have stood. There were no indications of a struggle. Mel Edmunds seemed to have obligingly turned his back on his killer. Hawker widened his search, checking bathroom, bedroom and dressing room for signs of theft or intrusion. Everything was in order.

The only possible mode of entry into the suite was through the main door. He crossed to it. After applying his eye to the peep-hole to make sure there was nobody outside, he opened the door and went cautiously out. To his right was a long stretch of carpeted corridor, running towards the lifts at the centre of the top floor. To his left was a much shorter corridor, terminating at a picture window that offered a breathtaking view of Monte Carlo. Adjacent to the window were double doors that gave access to the emergency exit.

Hawker ran to the doors to find them heavy and snug-fitting. He pushed his way through and looked at the concrete staircase which spiralled its way downwards through a series of fire doors at each level. Counting the steps, he walked down to the next floor then quickly came back up again. The corridor was still empty as he let himself into the suite once more. He moved slowly towards the sofa, then halted as soon as Mel's feet came into sight.

Something caught his attention. Beside the telephone on a mahogany side-table was a small leather address book. It lay open and face down. Hawker had not even noticed it when making his own panic call to the manager. As he picked the book up, he saw the initials of Mel Edmunds embossed in gold on the front. A flick through it showed him that all the names were female. He realized what he was holding. When he studied the page at which it had lain open, he noted four names.

One of them leapt straight up at him.

Lia Barelli.

The telephone number was in Cannes. Hawker could not understand why Mel should want to contact her. She belonged to his past. Unless his career as a playboy had continued *after* his marriage. He was overwhelmed with a sense of betrayal on Katie's behalf. She doted on her husband. The existence of the address book must be kept from her at all costs. He thrust it into his pocket.

Another priority now beckoned. Katie had to be prevented from coming up to the suite. News of Mel's death had to be broken to her as tactfully as possible. At all events, she must not be allowed to see the body in its gruesome condition. Hawker let himself out of the room again and trotted along the corridor to the lifts. There were six of them, two banks of three facing each other. He pressed all the call buttons before he became aware of the problem. As he descended to the ground floor, Katie Britwell might be on her way up in another lift. They would pass in transit.

Hawker was in a quandary. As an empty lift arrived and opened, he hesitated. Its doors closed soundlessly and it descended to a lower floor. His attention now switched to the indicator above one of the lifts opposite. It was climbing steadily up the building and came all the way to the top, stopping with a loud ping. When the doors parted, three men stepped out. Hawker guessed at once that the short, stout, balding man in the Pierre Cardin suit was the hotel manager.

'Mr Lequesne?'

'*Oui, M'sieur.*'

'I'm Don Hawker. I rang you a few minutes ago.'

'Come with us, please.'

'But I need to –'

'All in good time, M'sieur.'

Before he could object, Hawker was more or less swept along the corridor by the trio. The manager was a well-groomed, once-handsome man of middle years with a peremptory manner. His two companions were clearly members of the hotel security staff. In the time that it took them to get to the suite, Hawker explained how he had come to discover the body. Lequesne used a master card-key to gain entry. One of his men stayed outside in the corridor. The other – big, burly, impassive and watchful – followed the manager in. Hawker went after them and the door was shut behind them.

Lequesne blenched when he caught sight of the body.

'*Merde!*'

Moving with practised care, the security man bent down to carry out a quick examination of the corpse. He and the manager had a lengthy dialogue in French. Hawker was restive. His abiding concern was to protect Katie.

'Excuse me . . .' he began.

Lequesne turned on him with evident suspicion.

'Yes, M'sieur?'

'I must get to Mrs Edmunds at once,' argued Hawker. 'She was in the hairdressing salon. She may well be on her way up here now.' He gestured towards the body. 'We must spare her this.'

After a moment's consideration, the manager nodded. He walked to the telephone, snatched it up and dialled a number. When he got through, his tone was crisp and authoritative. He replaced the receiver and took a step towards Hawker.

36

'Madame Edmunds was about to leave. I have told them to detain her at the salon until you arrive.'

'Good.'

'You will need somewhere private.'

'What? . . . Oh, yes.'

'I will arrange something.' Lequesne picked up the telephone again. 'One of my staff will meet you at the salon.'

'Thanks.'

Hawker headed for the door but the manager's voice halted him.

'One thing, M'sieur . . .'

'Yes?'

'Don't try to leave the hotel, will you?'

The implication stung Hawker.

Katie Britwell was surprised when she was asked to wait in the salon. As the minutes ebbed away, her surprise turned to anxiety then degenerated into mild alarm. By the time Hawker came bustling in, she was on the verge of being seriously disturbed. She hurried across to meet him.

'Don, what's going on?'

'Nothing.'

'Then why was I kept here?'

'I'll explain it all,' he promised.

'Hey, is this some gag Mel's dreamed up?' she asked, trying to reassure herself. 'I know he's got a wacky sense of humour. Has Mel cooked up something special for me?'

Hawker struggled hard to sound calm and casual.

'No, Katie. Not exactly.'

'So what's happening?' She gave a nervous laugh. 'By the way, how do I look?'

'Mm?'

'I've just spent an hour in that chair, damn you!'

'Ah, yes.'

'Well?' She adjusted her hair with a hand.

'Terrific,' he murmured.

Her hair was beautifully coiffured and the face beneath it was glowing with a fragile joy. Katie Britwell was a true English rose. It pained Hawker that he had to be the one to crush her petals.

'M'sieur . . .'

A young woman in the pale blue uniform of a nurse came briskly into the salon. Hawker could see from her eyes that she knew.

'Follow me, please,' she invited.

'Right,' he said, taking Katie's arm.

'Where are we going?' asked Katie as she was led out.

'You'll soon see,' he told her.

They went along the corridor, turned left then stopped outside a door. The nurse unlocked it and ushered them in.

'I will be here if you need me, M'sieur,' she said.

Hawker nodded his thanks and closed the door. He and Katie were in the medical room. It was small, featureless and smelled faintly of disinfectant. A bed, two chairs and a cabinet stood against one wall.

Katie swung round to demand an explanation.

'What the hell is going on here!'

'Take it easy,' he advised.

'Why can't we go up to the suite?'

'There's been an accident.'

'Accident?'

'I'm afraid so.'

'What kind of accident?'

'Katie —'

'What *kind* of accident?' she demanded.

'The worst kind.'

'Mel?' Her face collapsed in anguish. 'Is he hurt bad?'

'Yes . . .'

'How bad?'

38

His expression was answer enough. Katie Britwell sagged visibly. Unable to cope with the horror of what she had been told, she tried to dismiss it with an hysterical giggle. She pushed him playfully.

'Go on. You're kidding me.'

'I wish I was.'

'This is some sort of weird joke.'

'No, Katie.'

'Mel? Dead? It's ridiculous!'

'He was murdered.'

His whisper was deafening. She put her hands to her ears and let out a scream of protest. Then she made a dive for the door. Hawker caught her and restrained her.

'Let me go!' she insisted. 'I must get up there.'

'Stay here.'

'I want to see for myself.'

'That's not possible.'

'Let me go!' she howled.

She beat on his chest with both fists but her struggle soon subsided. Falling against him, she began to sob convulsively. He almost carried her across to the bed, eased her into a sitting position, then settled down beside her. His soothing words went unheard. She was beyond consolation. Katie was locked in a private hell and had to submit to its fierce torments.

Hawker supported her with gentle firmness, wishing there was something he could do or say to comfort her. But there was not. His own experience had shown that. Some things could not be shared. You had to suffer them alone. He remembered it with searing clarity.

It was ten minutes or more before she calmed down enough to accept the offer of a handkerchief. Muttering to herself, she dabbed at her tear-stained face. Katie was desolate. She looked up at him.

'Don . . .'

'Yes?'

39

'Who could have *done* such a thing?'

'I'll find out.'

It was no idle boast. Hawker had made a sacred vow.

Chief Inspector Yves Daninos watched his forensic team at work. They were quiet, thorough, professional. The body which had brought them all to the Hotel Brassard still lay on the carpet in a pool of blood. Daninos sighed. A young champion had been cut down in his prime. The sense of waste rankled. So much potential would go unfulfilled.

Tall, wiry and wearing a blue mohair suit, Daninos had a decidedly professorial air. He looked as if he would be more at home in a lecture room than at a murder scene. A fastidious man, he was frankly appalled by the hideous mess on the floor. He would be glad when the corpse was taken away to the morgue. It unsettled him.

Sergeant Raoul Chabrier, by contrast, was unmoved. He gazed down at Mel Edmunds with detached interest. Chabrier was a sturdy man of medium height. It was impossible to mistake him for anything but a policeman. He wore his light grey suit as if it were the uniform of the Monagesque Gendarmerie. There was something solid and unforgiving about him. He would have no qualms about shooting to kill in the line of duty.

Daninos beckoned him across with a flick of the finger.

'*L'Anglais, Raoul.*'

'*Monsieur Hawker?*'

'*Oui.*'

'*Maintenant?*'

'*S'il vous plaît.*'

'*Ici?*'

'*Non. La chambre.*'

Chabrier nodded and went off on his errand. After a

last glance at the body, Daninos strode into the bedroom and left his *agents* to it. The bedroom had an exotic feel to it. The four-poster which occupied a central position had silk sheets. Ornate furniture contributed to the almost decadent mood. Large paintings of female nudes were mildly exciting without being in any way pornographic. The carpet was inches thick, the ceiling low and moulded, the light fittings superb. It was a room for lovers.

There was an upright armchair in front of the elaborate dressing table. Daninos turned it around to face into the room. Then he placed another chair close to it. Sitting on the edge of the bed, he took out a notebook and consulted it. Henri Lequesne had been voluble. The detective wanted to remind himself of everything that the manager had told him. When he had read through his notes, he turned his attention to the room itself.

The contents of the wardrobe and the chest of drawers gave him a lot of information about the occupants of the suite. Items left in the Gucci suitcases provided him with further clues. On one bedside table was a paperback novel by Jackie Collins. Some tennis magazines and a sailing manual lay on the other. Daninos leafed through the top magazine until he came to a photograph of Mel Edmunds. The player was in a characteristic pose. Close to the net during an indoor tournament in Memphis, Tennessee, he was stretching forward to play one of his feather-light drop shots. There was a balletic quality that appealed to Daninos. He read the caption then put the magazine aside.

Katie Britwell was featured on the cover of the next magazine. She looked both gorgeous and explosive, sweeping a ball down the line with a forehand volley, her features alight with sheer exhilaration. He was still admiring the picture when there was a knock on the door.

'*Entrez!*'

Chabrier escorted Hawker into the room.

Tossing the magazine on the bed, Daninos crossed swiftly to the Englishman to shake hands and perform the introductions. His voice was soft and cultured. His gaunt face bore a sad smile.

'How is Madame Edmunds?' he inquired solicitously.

'Devastated.'

'*Naturellement*. Someone is with her?'

'The hotel nurse.'

'Such a tragedy! We must do all we can to help.'

'The best way to help her,' suggested Hawker, 'is to leave her alone for the time being. Katie's wiped out.'

Daninos shrugged. '*C'est impossible, M'sieur*. I must see her.'

'Can't it wait until morning?'

'This is a murder investigation. Nothing waits.' He waved Hawker to the chair in front of the dressing table. 'Please, M'sieur. Make yourself comfortable.'

Hawker sat down but comfort was out of the question because Chabrier took the seat right next to him. His proximity was oppressive. The detective had not said a word during their journey to the top floor but he had somehow made Hawker feel under arrest. When Chabrier simply took out his notebook, there was a subtle menace in his movements. Dark eyes stared at Hawker from either side of a broken nose. The Frenchman could make the most innocent person experience guilt.

Daninos was altogether different. Friendly, open, unthreatening. He remained on his feet so that he could roam at will. He had the academic's harmless intensity.

'This is a most intriguing case,' he confided.

'Is it?' said Hawker.

'So many possibilities. A real challenge. Eh, Raoul?'

'*Oui*,' grunted his colleague.

'For instance,' continued Daninos, 'the killer may turn out to have been a hotel thief.'

'Thief?' repeated Hawker.

'He stole the dead man's wallet.'

'Ah.'

'Yet he left many other things of value.' The Chief Inspector pointed a bony finger. 'In that drawer behind you, M'sieur, there is a diamond necklace worth at least a hundred thousand francs. You see? Either he is a very stupid thief. Or a very special one. And another question. Why does Madame Edmunds leave her jewellery lying about in a drawer when there is a hotel safe? Already, we have complications.'

He picked up the magazine that lay on the bed and examined the front cover again. He strolled away from Hawker as he spoke.

'How long have you known her?'

'Katie?' Hawker shrugged. 'Four, five years.'

'You are close friends?'

'Not really. We don't see each other very often.'

'You would like to see more of her?'

'Well, yes.'

'How did the two of you meet?'

'In a television studio.'

'Really, M'sieur?'

'We took part in a programme together. A sports quiz.'

Daninos smiled. 'Did you win?'

'I didn't. Katie's team did.'

'And after that, you kept in touch with her.'

'On and off.'

The Chief Inspector turned to face him. They were on opposite sides of the room now. Chabrier was writing something in his notebook.

'Tell me about her,' invited Daninos.

'Katie Britwell is the best thing that's happened to British tennis for ten years,' said Hawker firmly.

43

'Probably since the war.'

'Tell me about her as a woman.'

'Nice girl. Lots of guts. Very independent.'

'Is she the romantic type?'

'I don't know about that.'

'What sort of book would you find by her bedside?'

'No idea.'

'Is she ambitious?'

'Oh, yes.'

'Intelligent?'

'Highly.'

'Was it a happy marriage?'

Hawker hesitated. 'I think so.'

'But you were their confidant.'

'Only for the last few days.'

'You must have sensed what was going on between them.'

'Up to a point.'

'Did she love her husband?'

'Very much.'

'Did you kill him?'

The question was all the more stunning because of the casual tone in which it was asked. Hawker reeled. He had been taken quite unawares. Anger mixed with indignation.

'No, I did not!'

'Is that the truth, M'sieur?'

'Of course!'

He rose to his feet but Chabrier restrained him with a hand on his arm. After a rueful glance at both of them, he sat down again. Daninos came across to him. His quizzical expression kept Hawker on the defensive. The latter spread his hands and shrugged his shoulders.

'What possible reason could *I* have to kill Mel Edmunds?'

'This one.'

44

The magazine was dropped into his lap. Katie looked up at him. Then something odd happened. Hawker realized for the first time just how much he disliked Mel. His sympathy had been entirely for her. He had hardly spared a thought for the deceased.

Daninos leaned over him like a surgeon about to operate.

'You found the body, M'sieur Hawker?'

'Yes.'

'Dead or alive?'

'Dead.'

They watched him carefully. He withstood their scrutiny.

Picking up the magazine again, Daninos went to replace it on the bedside table. He seemed disappointed. When he turned to face Hawker again, his affability had vanished. There was an edge to his voice.

'You were a famous athlete, I believe.'

'Long ago.'

'Forgive me, M'sieur. I know little of such things. I regard them as trivial.' He indicated his colleague. 'Raoul is our sportsman. I prefer the opera and the ballet. Are you interested in the arts?'

'No.'

'I thought not. Raoul tells me you were in the Moscow Olympics.'

'Montreal,' corrected Hawker.

'You won a gold medal.'

'Two.'

'Two gold medals. Even better. But they took them off you.'

Hawker winced as an old wound was reopened. After all these years, it still hurt. Time had not managed to dull the pain.

'They *tried* to take them off me,' he explained. 'I appealed against the decision and won.'

'It must have taken the shine off the medals.'

'I could certainly have done without the hassle.'

Daninos became businesslike. He strode back to confront Hawker.

'Describe your movements in the last two hours, please.'

'Two hours?'

'Be as exact as you can about times,' ordered the detective. 'It is important. Tell us everything you did, everyone you met.'

'I am ready, M'sieur,' said Chabrier, poised to write.

Hawker looked at his watch and assembled his thoughts.

'Two hours ago, I was back at my hotel. With Christina . . .'

He described it all in as much detail as he chose to remember. The encounter with Quentin Rivers was duly mentioned. Hawker never thought he would have cause to be grateful to the tennis correspondent but the latter was now part of the alibi which kept him out of Room 1250 during the likely time when the murder occurred. Chabrier wrote swiftly and without complaint. Daninos asked for clarification on a few points. Hawker eventually reached the end of his account.

The detectives conversed rapidly in French before switching their gaze back to him. Daninos fired another unexpected question.

'You are pleased that Monsieur Edmunds is dead?'

'Of course not!' protested Hawker.

'You did not like him, I think.'

'Mel was . . . fine.'

'Many people hated the man. He was very unpopular.' He gave a wry smile. 'Except with the ladies. That is often the case, I fear. They have a weakness for his type. Look at his wife.' He changed his tack. 'You say in your statement that you examined the body to see if it was still alive.'

'That's right.'

46

'Did you touch anything else?'

'Apart from the phone – no.'

'You didn't *take* anything, M'sieur?'

'Why should I?'

'Answer the question, please.'

'I find it insulting.'

'*Pardon*!'

The address book was burning a hole in Hawker's pocket. He sought to cover his embarrassment by going on the attack.

'How much longer do we play this game?' he demanded.

'Game?'

'Where you kid me along for a while then take a swipe at me with a question like that.'

'It is no game, *mon ami*.'

'Get off my back, will you?'

'Why?'

'Because I've told you all I know.'

'Maybe.'

'And because I resent being treated as the prime suspect.'

'But that is what you are,' said Daninos reasonably. 'Until we find another. You had the opportunity and the means. The motive, too, perhaps. Who knows? You had the key to the suite when Monsieur Edmunds was alone. It would take a strong arm to smash his skull like that. We can see how fit you like to keep yourself.'

'I did not kill him!' insisted Hawker.

'Someone did,' retorted Chabrier. 'And it is our job to find them. This is the independent sovereign state of Monaco. We set ourselves high standards, M'sieur. We do all we can to keep the crime rate down. We have problems, of course. But we do not usually have VIP's murdered in their hotels. It is – you will understand – not good for business. That is why we have to clear up this mess very quickly.'

47

There was a tap on the door. Chabrier went over to open it and exchanged a few remarks with another detective. He glanced across at Daninos who nodded in approval. Hawker gathered that they were asking permission to remove the corpse. Chabrier closed the door again and stood in front of it.

The Chief Inspector appraised him for a few moments.

'I think you do not enjoy your stay in Monaco.'

'Let's just say that I won't be in any rush to come back.'

'Too expensive?'

'That's part of it.'

'Too elitist?'

'So is that.'

'What is the main reason, M'sieur?'

'I prefer real people.'

'Hear that, Raoul?' said Daninos with amusement. 'He does not like us or our sunshine. Monsieur Hawker prefers London with its rain, its filth and its crime wave.'

'Every time,' confirmed Hawker.

'When did you plan to leave us, M'sieur?'

'Tomorrow morning.'

'Oh, no. That cannot be. We shall need you again.'

'But I have a flight booked,' argued Hawker.

'Postpone it.'

'I've got other commitments back in England.'

'You will stay here to help us with our inquiries.'

'Inspector, there's nothing else I can tell you!'

'Yes, there is,' returned Daninos. 'And it is *Chief* Inspector.'

'You can't keep me against my will,' said Hawker, rising.

'*Mais, non.* You will be staying at our request.'

'Suppose I refuse?'

'We shall confiscate your passport.' He put a hand

on Hawker's shoulder. 'Come now, M'sieur. Think of Madame Edmunds. You are her friend. You want her husband's killer to be caught, do you not?'

'Sure.'

'Then help us.'

Hawker was sardonic. 'Sign a confession, you mean?'

'*Très bien!*' Daninos gave a short laugh. 'I will let you into a secret, M'sieur. I do not believe it was you.'

'That's a relief.'

'You are too English for a *crime passionnel*.'

'Is that what this is?'

'We shall see.'

He offered his hand again and Hawker shook it reluctantly. The Chief Inspector took him slowly across the room. He might have been a professor talking to a student after a lecture.

'Monsieur Edmunds made enemies very easily.'

'Mel liked to speak his mind.'

'He also liked to bully people,' said Daninos. 'The rich are sometimes like that. Henri Lequesne, the manager, tells me that the hotel had nothing but trouble from this suite. Monsieur Edmunds would order room service then shout at the staff who came up here. His language was very crude. Very American.' They stopped by the door. 'He may have been a brilliant tennis player but he knew nothing about good manners. Or, indeed, about wine.'

'Wine?'

'The glass which was spilled on the carpet,' he explained. 'An inferior Sauvignon. Cheap and not nice. Such a poor choice for a man's last drink on earth.' He gestured to Chabrier who opened the door. 'You may go now, M'sieur.'

'Thanks.'

'Raoul will take you back down.'

'I can find my own way.'

'The media will be swarming all over the lobby by

now. They will pester you without mercy. Go with Raoul in the service lift. It will take you down to the kitchens. You will dodge them all.'

'Right.'

'*Au revoir, M'sieur.*'

'See you.'

'Oh, by the way . . .'

'What?'

'You didn't tell us *why* they tried to strip you of your Olympic gold medals.'

'No,' said Hawker brusquely. 'I didn't.'

He walked quickly out through the door.

Alain Dupont lay on a recliner beside his indoor swimming pool. He was naked beneath his multi-coloured beach robe. An empty glass stood on the low table beside him. He watched Dimitri as the latter cleaved his way through the water with lazy power. The swimmer's body was like that of a Greek god and Alain admired its sculptured smoothness. His young friend was very special. Like all the others.

The sound of a jingle took his eyes across to the portable colour television. A news programme was about to begin. The opening credits rolled up over film of the Hotel Brassard. Police cars could be seen clustered outside. The face of the newscaster appeared on the screen. He looked suitably shocked by the sensational news he had to pass on. Dimitri paused at the edge of the pool so that he could watch as well.

Mel Edmunds had been murdered. They showed film of his body being loaded into an ambulance. Chief Inspector Yves Daninos was laconic at the brief press conference. The police were pursuing their inquiries.

Alain's face glowed with wicked delight.

'Wonderful!' he breathed. 'Quite wonderful!'

'Good news? No?' said Dimitri.

'Indeed it is. I'm not a vindictive man but this does

give me a deep satisfaction. It's almost as if it's been laid on purely for my benefit.'

Dimitri grinned and brought his feet up to push himself off towards the centre of the pool. He floated on his back and savoured the moment. Bronzed and glistening, he looked even more like a young Adonis. It was a seductive image.

Alain stood up and slipped off his beach robe.

Then he executed a perfect dive into the water.

Guido Barelli was being driven to the Nice-Côte d'Azur International Airport when he heard the news on the car radio. Vincente took one hand off the wheel to turn up the volume. Barelli listened open-mouthed then let out a peal of laughter. Vincente contented himself with a quiet smile. His employer nudged his arm. A large foot went down on the accelerator and the Lamborghini shot away like a space rocket.

As soon as they reached the terminal building, the excited husband ran to the nearest public telephone and rang his wife in Cannes. They talked in high-speed Italian.

'Have you *heard*, my darling?' he asked.

'Heard what?'

'Mel Edmunds. He is dead.'

'Never!'

'He was murdered at the Hotel Brassard.'

'When? How?' Lia was flustered.

'What does it matter? The bastard is gone.'

'*Murdered*?'

'Someone smashed his skull in.'

There was an audible gulp from the other end of the line.

'This changes everything,' he said. 'Lia? Do you hear?'

'Yes, yes.'

'We can start again. Properly.'

'If you say so, Guido.'

'Aren't you *pleased*?'

A momentary pause. 'Yes, I am pleased.'

'I will ring you from Roma.'

'Right.'

'*Ciao, mio ben!*'

'*Ciao!*'

He put the receiver down and beamed all over again. When the news had sunk in, Lia had sounded happy. Barelli had not been able to see the tears in her eyes.

Yuri Chegenyov was dining in the restaurant at the Hotel Mirabeau. His manager had left him alone for a few minutes and the Russian was able to return some of the interest that was being shown in him by the lovely young Frenchwoman at the table in the corner. She had angled her seat so that she had a good view of him throughout the meal, and she had shot him meaningful glances on the few occasions that he had looked in her direction. Chegenyov was attracted to Western women but rarely able to indulge himself. Alex saw to that. He was manager, coach and moral guardian. Yuri found his lack of personal freedom irksome. There were times – like now – when he wanted to be rid of his human chastity belt.

Sex was so easy in the West. Tennis stars were always trailed by beautiful women. They could pick and choose. He envied the other players with an intensity that Alex would never have guessed at. Yuri Chegenyov did not just covet success. He wanted all the trappings that went with it.

Taking advantage of a rare opportunity, he looked across at his young admirer. She was chic, poised, in her early twenties. She smiled hopefully at him and he replied with a gentle nod. Their eyes locked across the restaurant and they conversed in the Esperanto of lust. It was time to become more closely acquainted.

Chegenyov got to his feet, put his napkin aside and made to leave the table.

But he was thwarted yet again. Alex Kutsk was bearing down on him. The stocky figure moved with speed and the big, blank face was for once animated.

They spoke in Russian and kept their voices low.

'Sit down, Yuri,' said his manager.

'But I was just —'

'Sit down.' Alex eased him back into his seat. 'I have something to tell you, Comrade. Something amazing.'

'Oh?'

'Do you know what I have just heard?'

Alex smirked as he broke the news about Mel Edmunds. The Russian player did not seem at all surprised and he did not pay the tribute of a passing sigh to his former adversary. Only one thing mattered to him.

'Now I will win Wimbledon!'

It was well after midnight before the police completed their first round of investigations at the Hotel Brassard. Katie Britwell did not want to be questioned at such length by Daninos but she knew that it was essential. There was vital information that only she could impart. The Chief Inspector was as courteous as the circumstances permitted. He applied no undue pressure. As he probed away, he sensed that Katie was holding something back but he was not sure if this was deliberate policy or the result of her confused state of mind. She told him the precise time when she had last seen her husband alive. During the hour she spent in the hairdressing salon, Mel Edmunds was battered to death.

The interview was held in the manager's office with Chabrier in attendance. Lequesne himself was busy circulating among his staff and guests, trying to impose some calm and still the ghoulish speculation. A murder on the premises was bound to have an adverse effect on the hotel. Damage limitation was the order of the day. Cruising around with a reassuring smile, he did his best to create an air of normality.

Hawker lingered until the police had finished. He wanted to be on hand in case Katie needed him. After some hesitation, she decided to spend the night at the hotel and another room was quickly prepared for her. A doctor prescribed a sedative and a uniformed gendarme was left outside her door. Since there was nothing more he could do, Hawker made for the exit.

A female voice hailed him from across the lobby.

'Don!'

'Yes?'

'Hold on a minute!'

Nance Paulson came trotting across to him. They knew each other by sight but had never really spoken before. The tragedy which had brought them both there dispensed with the need for introductions. They were both mourners.

'How is she?' asked Nance.

'Out on her feet.'

'Poor kid!'

'Katie doesn't know what hit her.'

'They wouldn't let me speak to her. I was going to try to persuade her to come back with me. We've got masses of room.'

'She just wants to be alone.'

'Oh, sure,' agreed Nance. 'But not *here*. I mean, this is where it happened, for Chrissake.'

'Fair point.'

'The associations are bound to get to her. She could have stayed with us and been among friends.' She touched his arm. 'Tell her that, won't you, Don? Say that I was here.'

'I will.'

'We'll do anything – anything at all – to help Katie.

Make sure she understands that. We're only two minutes away by car. Same goes for you, Don. You need anything, just yell out.'

'Thanks.'

'Katie knows where to find us.'

'Right.'

'You're welcome to a bed as well, if you want it.'

'Very kind of you, Nance.'

'Least I can do. Truth is, I feel so damn guilty.'

'Guilty?'

'Yeah,' said the other. 'Mel and Katie had dinner with us last night. Wanted them to meet this friend of ours. But Mel hated him on sight and didn't bother to keep it a secret. The party sure turned sour after that. My fault. Should've realized that he and Alain would never be big buddies. Feel so rotten about it.'

'Why?'

'Well!' she exclaimed. 'Put yourself in my shoes. Last time ever I see the guy socially, it's a total screw-up. Thanks to me.'

'With you now.'

'My husband went crazy after they'd all gone. Jean-Louis is very French. He believes that dinner with friends and good wine is the high point of civilization. Mel would never have got a second invite.' She heaved a sigh. 'Still, that's all water under the bridge. What we gotta do now is to rally round Katie. Don't forget my message.'

'I'll tell her,' he promised.

'Hey, you must be dead beat,' she said. 'Sorry to hold you up. Daresay you just wanna crawl off to the sack.' A thought nudged her. 'Say, you got transport? Car's outside if you need a lift.'

'No, thanks. It's not far.'

'Okay, then. Be seeing you, Don.'

'Cheerio . . .'

They went out through the main door together then

Nance struck off towards the car-park. Hawker went down the steps and headed towards the boulevard. Two men were talking in the shadow of a palm tree. One of them stepped out as he approached.

'I did warn you, old boy,' he mocked.

It was Quentin Rivers. Complacent, triumphant, patronising.

'Good-night,' said Hawker pointedly.

'I said it wouldn't last.'

'Do you read the tea leaves as well?'

'Your story just died on you, Hawker.'

'Piss off.'

Hawker pushed past him and walked swiftly down the drive.

'Find another sport to inflict yourself on!' called Rivers.

Derisive chuckles came from under the palm tree but they went unregarded. Hawker was preoccupied with other matters. He had lied to Nance Paulson. His hotel was almost a mile away. There were two reasons why he declined her offer of a lift. He wanted to be on his own and he felt uneasy in her company. Nance was over-eager to help. It could be put down to genuine concern but there was an aggressive curiosity as well, and he was in no mood to cope with it.

He reviewed what had been a very full day. The early morning run. Breakfast with Christina. Accumulated drama at the final against Chegenyov. Celebrations. Farewell scene at his hotel. Going out to dinner. Quentin Rivers. The salon. Opening the door. Finding the body. Calling the manager. Telling Katie. Facing the police. Lying to them. Waiting interminably. Nance. Rivers again.

Questions lapped at his mind. Why did Katie miss part of the match? What gave Mel the impetus to win? Did he ring Lia Barelli? Who killed him? What was the motive? And the murder weapon? Why was his wallet

56

stolen? How did the killer escape from the hotel?

Why did Katie Britwell marry him in the first place?

The protracted traumas of the evening had left him exhausted and he was grateful for the cool night air. He wanted nothing so much as to turn his back on it all and feel the welcoming arms of Christina Erikkson around him, but she had flown off to Hamburg some hours ago. He was going back to a lonely room in a small and unfashionable hotel. Settling back into the usual pattern of his life.

Monte Carlo was a place of winking lights and swaying palm trees. The casino, the clubs and the discos were in full swing. Music carried by the wind indicated that there were parties aboard some of the yachts. While Mel Edmunds lay dead, people continued to enjoy themselves. It only served to distance Hawker even more from the glittering princedom. His strongest urge was to get right away but he had to stay at the express command of the police. It was irksome.

When he finally reached the hotel, he pressed the night bell to rouse the night porter, a taciturn old man with a cigarette stuck in the corner of his mouth. Admitted to the lobby, the guest was given a message with his key. The slip of paper bore a Hamburg number. While the porter wrestled with the switchboard, Hawker squeezed himself into the tiny booth which housed the public telephone. He lifted the receiver. After a couple of false starts, the porter got through. The number rang out for a long time.

Then he heard a voice he had come to cherish.

'Hawker?'

'Did I wake you up?'

'I was in the bath.'

'Good.'

'I only went in there to stay awake.' She sounded peeved. 'Look at the time! Where have you *been*?'

57

'Long story.'

'I heard the news on the radio. That's why I rang.'

'Thanks, Christina.'

'How are you?'

'Been a hell of an evening.'

'Tell me everything.'

'Can't afford the phone bill.'

'But they gave no details on the radio,' she said. '*How* was Mel Edmunds killed? Don't keep me in suspense.'

'I'll give you the shortened version.'

He recounted what had happened from the moment he entered the penthouse suite at the Hotel Brassard. Christina listened intently and gasped in surprise from time to time. By the end of the story, her sympathies were flowing freely.

'Poor man!' she said. 'What a terrible way to die!'

'Mel didn't know too much about it.'

'I feel so sorry for Katie. A blow like that!'

'Pole-axed her.'

'They'd only been married – what? – six, seven months.'

'Lot of that time was spent apart,' he reminded.

'It's so cruel! Oh, my heart goes out to her!'

'Mine, too.'

'She lived for Mel.'

'Katie's going to need a lot of help to get through this.'

'I'm not sure that she ever will. I wouldn't.' She shifted her concern to him. 'But what about you, Hawker?'

'Me? Oh, I'm fine.'

'After *that*?'

'Bit bruised, maybe.'

'I hadn't realized you were the one who found the . . . It must have been such a shock. To walk in on him like that.'

'Real kick in the stomach.'

'Then all that shit from the police.'

'Last thing I need.'

'It just doesn't make sense,' said Christina, trying to puzzle it out. 'Why would anyone want to kill Mel Edmunds?'

'He had his enemies.'

'Yes,' she conceded. 'When you're number one, you'll never be favourite with the others. They're as jealous as hell. But that doesn't mean to say they'll smash your head in.' She pondered. 'Do you think, maybe, it was an accident?'

'Accident?'

'Mel came in and found an intruder. There was a struggle and –'

'No, Christina,' he said firmly. 'It was no accident. This was cold-blooded murder by someone he knew and trusted.'

'*Knew?*'

'Mel would never have let them into the room otherwise,' argued Hawker. 'You know what he was like about privacy. There was a peep-hole in the door. He could see that it was a friend.'

'Some friend!'

'It does narrow the field a little.'

'Field?'

'The murderer is part of the tennis scene. Mel hardly knows anyone outside it. My guess is it's someone who was involved with the championship.'

'Another player? No, Hawker!'

'Passions run high in the game.'

'I know but . . .'

'Christina, will you do me a favour?'

'Of course.'

'Those photos you took today,' he said. 'You must have had some shots of the crowd.'

'Dozens of them.'

'Could you send me copies, please?'

'If you wish. But why do you –'

'Just send them. It's important.'

'That London address you gave me?'

'Yes. Soon as you can.'

'Okay.'

'You're beautiful.'

'Am I?' she fished. 'How beautiful?'

'Fly straight back and I'll tell you.'

'Miss me?'

'A little,' he teased.

'It was good,' she said wistfully. 'Very good. I was looking forward to Rome. Seeing you again. Now it's all off.'

'Why?'

'With Mel Edmunds out, you'll have no reason to go. And Katie won't be playing, that's for sure.'

'Don't worry, Christina,' he reassured. 'I'll be there.'

Hawker was more than ever convinced that the killer was part of the tennis circus. He would catch up with him if he had to follow the players all season. How ever long it took, he would see it through to the end.

'And me?' asked Christina, stifling a yawn.

'I'll be in touch.'

'Big kiss.'

'Take care.'

'Until Rome.'

'Don't forget the photos.'

'So long, Hawker.'

'And thanks . . .'

He came out of the booth and waved a farewell to the porter, who was lighting another cigarette. Hawker went upstairs and let himself into his room. After the palatial suite at the Hotel Brassard, it seemed more cramped and basic than ever. He slipped off his coat, tossed it over a chair and then flopped down on the bed.

Talking to Christina had both cheered and

depressed him. It was wonderful to hear her voice again but painful to realize that he would not see her for some time. She had brightened his stay in Monaco in ways he would never have imagined. Young, uncomplicated and totally free of inhibitions, she was able to rescue him from his easy-going melancholy. Christina Erikkson was exactly the tonic he needed. He was already suffering from withdrawal symptoms.

Weariness and dejection crept up on him. It was time to put the horrific event behind him. He removed his tie and picked at the buttons on his shirt before coming to an abrupt halt. Something flickered in his memory and banished his fatigue at once. Crossing to his coat, he felt in his pocket for the address book.

He studied it for a moment. Its very existence was a sad comment of the marriage. Like Katie, he believed that Mel had repented of his former ways. The playboy life had been publicly renounced at their wedding. It now looked as if Mel might have clung to it in private.

Hawker turned to the crucial page. Four names, four possibilities. Mel had been about to ring one of them. They were listed alphabetically. There was order in his love life.

Patti Baff. Lia Barelli. Jody Beecher. Ingrid Bellinghausen.

The name of Lia Barelli once again claimed his attention. It had to be her. Patti Baff was an Australian player. There were two numbers against her name, one in Melbourne, the other in London. Jody Beecher was a rising young star of the women's circuit. Still in her teens, she was based in Texas. Ingrid Bellinghausen was another American, a lean, leggy Californian with no less than three telephone numbers – in Los Angeles, New York and Miami. There must have been a time when Mel had been anxious to get in touch with her.

Lia Barelli set herself apart from the others in

various ways. She was by far the most attractive. She was not a tennis player. She possessed a husband. She had – according to rumour – a serious affair with Mel immediately before his marriage. There was an element of real danger about her. And she was within easy reach. Patti Baff, Jody Beecher and Ingrid Bellinghausen were all thousands of miles away. Lia was in Cannes. She had actually watched the final and seen her former lover revive his fortunes.

Had their proximity revived something else?

Hawker went back to the front of the book and flicked through the names. Mel Edmunds was certainly catholic in taste. A whole range of nationalities was represented. He had a girl in every port and a few more waiting on the substitutes' bench. Hawker recognized many of the names from the tennis world but there were several whom he could not place. He turned a page and glanced through another trio.

His eyes popped as he saw the last name he had expected.

Nance Paulson.

Chapter Three

Robert Alexander was awakened in his Kensington flat by the sound of the six o'clock news. The main item concerned the latest crisis in the Middle East and it gave him time to wipe the sleep out of his eyes. The murder of Mel Edmunds was in second spot and a few additional details had been released by the police in Monaco. Robert memorized every word. He was not pleased to learn that Don Hawker had discovered the body. When the newscaster moved on to a bomb blast in Northern Ireland, Robert reached out to silence the radio alarm.

Leaping out of bed with alacrity, he crossed to the window to draw the curtains and view the new day. Drizzle was falling out of a swollen sky but it did not dampen his spirits. He smiled as if he were basking in bright sunshine. Robert was a dark, slim, sleek man in his middle thirties with the unmistakable stamp of a leading public school on him. Even after a night in bed, his curly hair looked well-groomed. Over-conscious of his lack of height, he always stood bolt upright. He slipped off his pyjama jacket and went through his morning exercises. Then he headed for the bathroom.

Half an hour later, his dapper figure was striding purposefully through the drizzle towards the local newsagent's shop. There was a light on inside and signs of activity. The newsagent was a stocky, weathered individual in his fifties with the look of an ex-sailor.

Unshaven at that hour, he was busy marking a pile of papers with a pencil. He glanced up in surprise when Robert entered. Gums were bared in welcome.

'Blimey!'

'Good-morning, Sam.'

'You're up early, Mr Alexander.'

'Yes.'

'Just about to do your road,' said the newsagent. He found a copy of the *Times* and handed it over. 'One less for the boy to deliver.'

'Actually, I'd like some other papers as well.'

'Take your pick, sir.'

'One of each.'

'*All* of them?'

'Please, Sam.'

'Coming up,' said the other, sorting them out from the display on the counter. 'Got a special interest or something?'

'No.'

'You in the papers yourself, then? That it?'

'Nothing like that, Sam.'

'Just wondered, sir.'

'How much do I owe you?'

Robert paid for the papers then took his leave.

He walked briskly back to the flat, let himself in and went up to the third floor. Once inside his living room, he dropped down on the sofa and got to work. Mel Edmunds had made the front page in six papers. Three carried a full obituary and a fourth had a photo montage of his successes. Robert was absorbed. He was particularly interested in any mention of Katie Britwell. Several of the papers carried photos from the wedding album and one showed her winning a tournament in Birmingham.

It was the picture in the *Independent* that appealed to Robert. Taken at the Monte Carlo Open, it showed the victor holding up his trophy while his adoring wife stood at his side. Katie was beaming with pleasure. Robert stared at her for a long time then went into the kitchen to find a pair of scissors. When he came back, he lay the paper on the floor so that he could get at it. The photograph was carefully cut out and held up for examination. It had one grave defect.

Mel Edmunds.

Robert scissored him off without compunction then scrunched him up into a tiny ball. The reigning Wimbledon Men's Singles champion was thrown into the wastepaper basket. Katie Britwell was free at last.

She was now smiling at Robert Alexander.

Don Hawker went for his morning run, took a shower, missed Christina and ate a frugal breakfast. Without explaining why, he told the manageress that he might need his room for another night and she acceded to his request with a Gallic shrug. As soon as he was able, he fought his way into the telephone booth to make a series of calls.

The first was to the Hotel Brassard to check on Katie. Expecting to get no further than the switchboard, he was amazed when he was put straight through to her room.

'How are you?' he asked.

'Still a bit dopey. The sedative knocked me right out.'

'Probably the best thing for you, Katie.'

'Maybe.' Her speech was slow, almost slurred. 'Listen, Don. Can   you before I go?'

'Go where?'

'Back home. My father's arriving this morning. We fly off to London straight after lunch.'

'Has Chief Inspector What's-his-name finished with you?'

'No,' she said wearily. 'He's calling here for another

chat in about half an hour. I could do without that, I can tell you.'

'I know the feeling.'

'Can you come?' It was important to her.

'Just give me a time.'

'Twelve?'

'I'll be there.'

'That'll give you a chance to meet Daddy.'

'Good.' He remembered something. 'By the way, Nance Paulson was at the hotel last night. Wanted to know if there was anything she could do to help.'

'Yes,' said Katie dully. 'Nance rang first thing this morning. I've had lots of other callers as well. Didn't speak to any of them. You're the only person I can bear to talk to.'

'Thanks.'

'See you at twelve.'

'On the dot. Oh, Katie . . .'

'Yes?'

'You don't happen to have Nance Paulson's number, do you?'

'Why?' A defensive note intruded.

'No particular reason,' he said casually. 'Just wanted to ask her a small favour, that's all.'

Mel's address book had only furnished Nance's telephone number in Boston. He did not have details of her European base.

'I do have the number,' admitted Katie, 'but it's still up in the other room. They haven't brought my things down yet. But if you really need to get hold of Nance, look her up in the directory. Under her married name. Croizier. Her husband is Jean-Louis Croizier.'

'I'll do that.'

'Goodbye, Don.'

She hung up before he could say another word.

Hawker next got in touch with the airport to ask about the possibility of changing to a later flight.

Again, he met a pleasant surprise. He was put directly through to a helpful young woman who assured him that his ticket would be valid on another flight providing there was a seat available. It was one problem off the worry list.

The hotel switchboard had some difficulty connecting his third call but he eventually heard the gravel voice of his employer.

'Fretton.'

'It's me,' said Hawker.

'At last, you old bugger!'

'I'll make this quick, Eric. You're paying.'

'What's going on?' demanded Eric Fretton. 'They had a picture of you on breakfast telly this morning. I sent you down there to watch tennis not to get involved in a murder.'

'I had no choice.'

'So what gives?'

'The police want me to stay for a day or two.'

'Bollocks to that!'

'I'm grounded, Eric.'

'But you're supposed to be covering that squash tournament at Wembley this evening.'

'I told them.'

'Tell them again,' ordered Eric. 'Louder.' A thought nudged him. 'Hey, you're not in police custody, are you?'

'No,' said Hawker gratefully. 'They've given up believing that I actually killed Mel. They just don't think I've told them all I can.'

'Well, they're right there,' observed the other with a cackle. 'Don Hawker. The silent service. You play your cards so close to your chest that they're behind your sodding back.'

'Ready for the bad news, Eric?'

'There's *more*?'

'I want to stay with this story.'

'What story!' spluttered the editor. 'You were supposed to get the low-down on their marriage. Does screwing Katie Britwell three times a night ruin your serve – that kind of thing. There *is* no marriage now. They got divorced last night. The cheap way.'

'Eric, I'm on to something.'

'Big deal!'

'I must follow it through.'

'Not on my money.'

'Hear me out, will you?'

'No.'

'Mel Edmunds was murdered by someone on the tennis scene. The only way to find that person is from the inside. It's a small, incestuous, self-contained world. I need to stick around in it.'

'This is a sports magazine,' insisted Eric. 'Not a branch of Scotland Yard. Leave the sleuthing to the bloodhounds, Hawker. Get on the first plane you can and come back.'

'I'm serious, Eric.'

'So am I.'

There was an awkward pause. Neither man wanted to split up a working relationship that had been so enjoyable and productive over the years. They were good friends. They had immense respect for each other. A few hasty words could alter all that.

'Think it over,' suggested Hawker. 'That's all I ask.'

Eric Fretton was a hard-nosed editor. Only one thing counted.

'What's in it for the mag?'

'Best exclusive we've ever had.'

'Who Killed Cock Robin?'

'How marriage led to murder.'

'Come again.'

'It's the story you asked for in the first place, Eric. What makes them tick? When I know the answer, I'll tell you who the killer was.'

68

'You serious?'

'Put it this way,' said Hawker. 'If Mel Edmunds hadn't married Katie Britwell, he'd probably be alive today.'

There was a long silence. A one-man editorial conference was in progress. Hawker eventually broke in on it.

'Eric?'

'Shut up!'

'What's going on?'

'You bastard, Hawker.'

'Eh?'

'You got me interested.'

'Let me go to the Italian Open as planned.'

'And if that doesn't do the trick?'

'On to Paris for the French Open.'

'Yes,' moaned Eric. 'Then on to Queen's Club, then Wimbledon and so on. If you come good, we got an explosive story. If you fail, we move a giant step closer to the bankruptcy court.'

'Does that mean I go ahead?'

'Damn you, Hawker!' snarled Eric Fretton.

The conversation was over. Hawker had talked him around.

Another guest was waiting to use the telephone now so Hawker let him have the booth while he repaired to the local directory. With the aid of the manageress, he found the two numbers he was after. When the other guest vacated the booth, Hawker slipped into it again. He was put through to Nance Paulson. She could not have been more pleased to hear from him. When he tried to ask her some questions, she pressed him to come to the house. They could talk at length and in comfort there. Hawker made arrangements then rang off.

He was feeling much more sanguine now. Four phone calls had produced positive results. Katie

Britwell. The airport. Eric Fretton. Nance Paulson. So far, so good. He should have known that his luck would not last.

'*Si?*'

'Is that Mrs Barelli?'

'No!'

'Signora Lia Barelli?' he asked, venturing into raw Italian.

'Who is this?'

'My name is Hawker. Don Hawker.'

He had got off on the wrong foot. No fashion model operated under her married name. When she was adorning the front cover of *Vogue* or *Elle*, she was known simply as Lia. It was a name that had instant currency in her world.

'I'm a journalist,' he said. 'I covered the tennis tournament.'

'Guido is not here,' she snapped.

'As a matter of fact —'

'He go to Roma yesterday.'

'I wanted to talk to you.'

'*Why!*'

He faced two problems. Her manner was hostile and her English was only marginally better than his Italian. It was going to be sticky.

'I'm a friend of Mel Edmunds.'

'Who you say?'

'Mel Edmunds.'

'Not know him,' she said dismissively.

'But you watched your husband play him.'

'Guido want me there.'

'You sat through the final when Mel beat Chegenyov.'

'Mel Edmunds nothing to me.'

'Nothing at all?'

'Just another player.'

'When did you first meet him?'

70

'Why these questions?' she asked, bridling.

'You must have seen a lot of Mel around the circuit.'

'I no watch much. Only when Guido play.'

'Look,' he said, tiring of her evasion. 'You do know what happened at the Hotel Brassard last night, don't you? Mel was battered to death.'

A measured pause. The first hint of softness in her voice.

'I know,' she conceded.

'How does it make you feel?'

'I sorry.'

'Anything else?'

'Stop this!' she yelled, suddenly angry again.

'There's something I have to ask you.'

'You ask too much questions.'

'Please – it's very important.'

'I no speak more.'

'Did Mel ring you yesterday evening?'

There was a fierce snort of protest that banged at his ear-drum.

'You leave me alone. Ha!'

'Mrs Barelli . . .'

'What you say your name?'

'Don Hawker.'

'You no bother me, Mr Hawker. I tell Guido. I tell police. Mel is dead. I say nothing. Go away. *Capisco!*'

She slammed the receiver down to emphasize her point.

Hawker swallowed hard then came out of the booth. Lia Barelli was denying an intimate relationship – even a close acquaintance – with Mel Edmunds, and she was doing so with such vehemence that she confirmed all the rumours about them. Behind her show of temper was a sense of loss. Behind her threats was an admission that Hawker's questions were too close for comfort.

The other phone calls had been far more pleasant

but he suspected that this one might turn out to be the most revealing.

Jean-Louis Croizier finished a late breakfast and dabbed at his lips with the napkin. His normal geniality had been sabotaged by irritation.

'Who is this fellow?' he said.

'Don Hawker.'

'The man Katie was talking about?'

'That's him,' said Nance. 'He was an Olympic athlete who took up journalism when his running days were over. Katie's always had a soft spot for him. Don's a pretty straight guy.'

'Maybe. But do you have to invite him here?'

'He wanted to talk about Mel.'

'*Exactement*!'

'Hey!' she soothed, running a hand over his shoulder. 'Don't be like that, Jean-Louis. Okay, Mel could be a pain when he wanted to be.'

'The man was a pig!' he urged. 'An animal!'

'Never speak ill of the dead.'

'You forget what he *did* the other evening?'

'No,' she said evenly. 'Nor forgiven it either.'

'He insulted our guests, Nance. To their faces.'

'Yeah, I know.'

'There are standards. There are *rules*.'

'Mel always did like to overstep the mark.'

'He deserved what he got!'

'Jean-Louis!'

'Don't ask me for sympathy.'

Nance looked up as the doorbell rang in the distance.

'Here he is,' she noted. 'It might be better if you two didn't meet. I didn't mean to upset you by bringing him here.'

'That is okay. I will be going soon.'

'The office?'

'A board meeting.'

'That means you'll be late back again.'

She gave him an absent-minded kiss on the head and went out of the room. When she got to the verandah, the maid was already showing Hawker to a chair. Nance took over and they settled down together at a white wrought-iron table. A glance was enough to send the maid off to make a pot of coffee.

'Good of you to see me at such short notice,' he said.

'I meant what I said last night, Don.'

'You and Katie have been friends for some time, haven't you?'

'As much as tennis professionals *can* be friends,' she observed. 'We're rivals on court and we can never forget that. I guess it was the same in athletics. You never pal up with the guys liable to beat you.'

'Out on the track, I used to hate their guts,' he confessed.

'The killer instinct.'

The phrase popped out before she could stop it. There was a moment of shared embarrassment then Nance sailed on past it.

'Have you spoken to Katie?'

'No,' he lied.

'The hotel said she wasn't taking calls.'

'Understandable.'

'The kid needs moral support,' argued Nance. 'People like you or me around. She mustn't be left to brood at a time like this.'

'Brooding has its place,' he murmured.

'So what's the next step for Katie?'

'I don't know. Back home, I suppose.'

'The apartment in New York?'

'Hardly. To her parents, probably.'

'They're great,' she said. 'As English as they come and none the worse for it. I loved them both.'

Hawker appraised her. He had always admired her

as a player. It took enormous talent and application to dominate the women's game the way that Nance Paulson had. She was the ultimate professional. As a woman, however, she was less appealing. Nance was certainly vivacious but her moneyed self-confidence troubled him. There was a hardness to her manner that never quite disappeared.

'Okay,' she offered. 'Fire away.'

'What?'

'You said you had a few questions for me.'

'Oh, yes. That's right.' He wondered what she was thinking behind the smile. 'How long did you know Mel?'

'We go way back, Don. To the junior leagues.'

'What was he like in those days?'

'Much the same.'

'An eye for the ladies?'

'You bet!' she laughed. 'That guy was horny from birth. We had this joke about him. Only reason Mel played tennis was that it was easy to look up our skirts. Except that he wasn't content simply to look. He had to try to nail everything.'

'How well did you know him?'

'Not too well,' she replied. 'There was a time – after we both turned pro – when he tried to get me to play mixed doubles with him. I stuck it for a while but it just didn't work out.'

'Why not?'

'Look at the guy. He was essentially a singles player.'

'How would you rate him, Nance?'

'The best,' she said loyally. 'Quite simply the best. Mel was pure genius. Touch players like that only come along once in a blue moon. Most of us have to do it the hard way.'

Coffee arrived on a silver tray and the maid poured out two cups as directed. Both had milk but neither took sugar. Hawker sipped his coffee and waited till

74

the maid had withdrawn.

'Nance . . .'

'Ask it, Don.'

'Eh?'

'You wanna know why the hell they got married to each other.'

'Yes.'

'If you ever find out, let me know. I can't figure it out.'

'Katie was engaged to someone else.'

'That was more for his benefit than hers,' said Nance briskly. 'Drew had his good points but who wants to share their life with Mr Nice Guy? There was no sparkle in him. Mel was *all* sparkle.'

'What happened to Drew Grant?'

'What happens to most rejected lovers, I guess. They find someone else and screw themselves silly. Not that he's forgotten Katie, mind you. Drew could never do that. He's the torch-carrying type.'

Hawker had some more coffee then put his cup on the table.

'Those stories about Lia Barelli . . .'

'All true,' she asserted. 'No question of it.'

'Didn't her husband *know*?'

'Guido was too busy doing his own stallion routine. Those guys are two of a pair. Can't keep their zippers up.' Her mouth tightened. 'God knows why they bother with rackets when they play each other. They could hit the ball to and fro with their dicks. There's symbolism for you!' She gave a half-smile of repentance. 'Sorry. That was crude.'

'Wasn't Mel taking a big risk?'

'That was the turn-on,' she said. 'I mean, have you seen Vincente? The Barelli bodyguard? You don't keep someone like him around just to crack walnuts for you. He'd have snapped Mel in two.'

'The affair with Lia was *before* the marriage to Katie.'

She looked him full in the eye and her scepticism showed.

'Are you asking me to believe that Mel could be faithful?'

'Point taken.' Once again, Hawker suffered a pang on Katie's behalf. 'Tell me about that dinner party,' he invited.

'Here? It was some evening . . .'

Nance gave him a brief outline of what had happened and how the other guests had reacted. The blame was placed squarely on Mel. Hawker pricked up his ears at the mention of the phone call which had flustered Katie. He sought to link it with her absence from the early stages of the final. Perhaps Katie had been summoned away.

'She told me the call was from her father,' recalled Nance.

'In Paris?'

'Unlikely.'

'That's where she said she'd been.'

'Why, Don?'

'I don't know,' he answered. 'But she must have had a hell of a good reason to miss an occasion like that. Mel in with a chance of winning the championship. Needing her support.' He looked across at her. 'How would you feel if your husband did that to you, Nance?'

'I'd leave him,' she said crisply.

'As long as you came back, *ma chère.*'

Jean-Louis entered on cue. Posing on the step behind them, he wore a fawn suit with a brown tie and carried a brown document case. Nance introduced the two men and Hawker stood for the handshake.

'I never miss the big tournaments,' explained the Frenchman.

'He wouldn't dare!' joked Nance.

'I like to think my presence is a help.'

76

One arm around his wife, Jean-Louis was relaxed, urbane and affectionate but Hawker still heard the alarm bells. The smile did not reach the man's eyes which were cold, shrewd and merciless.

Hawker shuddered inwardly. He was not welcome. Jean-Louis Croizier was much more than a powerful businessman and an attentive husband. There was an air of civilized brutality about him. He was the sort of man who – if sufficiently upset – would have you killed by discreet arrangement.

Nance Paulson was not sharing her *life* with Mr Nice Guy.

Gerald Britwell was a big man who had been shrunk by age, illness and setback. Now in his early sixties, his hair had a Bardic whiteness and his shoulders had a pronounced stoop. He wore rimless spectacles to which a small hearing-aid was attached behind one ear. A retired accountant, he looked and dressed the part.

As soon as he entered the room at the Hotel Brassard, he put his arms out to enfold his daughter. They stood in a long, consoling embrace with silent tears being shed by both of them. Gerald kissed her softly on the forehead.

'Thanks for coming, Daddy,' she whispered.

'It was the earliest flight I could get.'

'I'm so glad to see you.'

'Your mother sends her love. She wanted to come with me.'

Katie nodded then indicated the sofa. They crossed to sit down. She used a handkerchief to wipe away tears from eyes that had done more than their share of crying in the past twelve hours or so.

'Would you like something to drink?' she offered.

'Not yet, darling.'

'Tea? Coffee?'

'I can wait.'

He held her hand and squeezed it gently. Katie's roving lifestyle meant that he rarely saw her for more than a couple of months a year. It was heart-breaking to find her in such distress. She looked small, bewildered and desperate.

'Do you want to talk about it?' he invited.

'What is there to say, Daddy?'

'You could try telling me how you feel.'

Shaking her head, she pursed her lips to hold back more tears.

'Do the police have any leads?'

'I don't know.'

'I'll want to speak to them before I leave.'

'Chief Inspector Daninos is still at the hotel.'

'Have they treated you well?'

'Very well.'

'If only I'd been *here*!' he sighed.

Katie lowered her head. Something was troubling her.

'Daddy . . .'

'Yes, darling?'

'Don't blame me, will you?'

'Of course not.'

'I know you didn't like Mel.'

'It wasn't that.'

'I know how much I hurt you and Mummy.'

'You loved him,' he soothed. 'That's all that matters.'

'Yes.'

Katie tried to shake off her grief. She asked about relatives and friends and pretended to look forward to going home again. It was just like old times. Returning to base after a long holiday. Gerald played along, talking with forced joviality, telling her about the new dog, the garden and bridge sessions with the neighbours. Little had changed in his life. The drama lay entirely with Katie.

Their conversation looped round on itself and they

were soon confronted once more with the horror that had brought them together. As delicately as he could, Gerald asked for details. Katie yielded them in a daze. Her father was suddenly seized by a fit of coughing and she had to comfort him. He apologized with a wan smile.

'I think I'd like a cup of tea now, Katie.'

'And me.'

She rang for room service then rejoined him on the sofa.

'I promised to pass on a message,' he said.

'Message?'

'Drew Grant.'

'Oh.'

'He sends his condolences.'

'Thank you.'

'And his love.'

Gerald watched hopefully but Katie was non-committal.

Guido Barelli rolled over with a groan of contentment and lay on his back. The girl nestled up to him and buried her cheek in the dark forest of his chest. It was still heaving from his exertions. They were in the bedroom of a luxury apartment in the most fashionable area of Rome. Sunlight was slanting in through the open window to stroke their naked bodies with warm fingers.

They spoke in Italian. Francesca had a mellifluous voice.

'Welcome home!' she said.

'Thanks.'

'I thought about you.'

'It was worth waiting.'

'What is your excuse for being in Roma this time?' she asked.

'My mother is sick.' He jabbed her playfully when she laughed. 'It is not an excuse, Francesca. Mama really is ill.'

'Seriously?'

'Her heart. She needs to lose weight and slow down.' He ran a hand down the curve of her body. 'Let's not talk about her.'

'I want to see more of you.'

'That is how it should be.'

'I mean it, Guido.'

'But you would tire of me if it happened too often.'

'Never,' she purred.

'Besides, I would only get in the way of your career.'

'Ha!' She was scornful. 'What career? The telephone has not rung for weeks and weeks. They have forgotten me, Guido.'

'Nobody could do that, my angel.'

Francesca was one of many young Italian actresses whose careers smouldered from time to time without ever catching fire. She tended to get small, decorative parts in films and the occasional supporting role in television. Guido Barelli helped to ease the boredom of resting.

She raised her head to place it beside his.

'Does your wife know about me?'

'Lia? No.'

'But she suspects?'

'Forget about her, my sweet.'

'Where is she now?'

'In Cannes.'

'And Vincente?'

'I left him there as well.' He smiled and pulled her close. 'I did not think I would need a bodyguard here.'

'He is such a *big* man,' she said dreamily.

'What about me?'

'Oh, you are big, too, Guido. But he is frightening. I like it.'

'Would you rather *he* was here now?' he asked jealously.

'Don't be silly.'

'Perhaps I should send Vincente next time.'

'I prefer you, my love,' she insisted. 'In every way.'

'Are you sure?'

She kissed him by way of reply. It was a long, luscious moment and he started to rouse again. Pulling her on top of him, he used both hands to draw slow circles on her buttocks. She saw him smirk.

'What is so funny?'

'I was thinking of the priest.'

'At a time like *this*?'

'He will be angry with me at confession.'

'Why?'

'Because I am not a dutiful son.' The smirk became a full grin. 'I am *glad* that Mama is ill. It brings me to you.'

They laughed together then locked in a fiercer embrace.

Hawker liked him. Gerald Britwell was harmless, well-meaning and rather ineffectual. There was a facial resemblance to Katie but he had none of her exuberance. For his part, Gerald turned out to be a devoted fan.

'I remember you winning the 5,000 at the Commonwealth Games.'

'Seems like a century ago.'

'You dogged that New Zealander for lap after lap then left him standing over the last hundred metres.' He chuckled at the memory. 'It was a typical Don Hawker race. You stayed with the pace then changed gear at the crucial moment.'

'It hurt,' recalled Hawker. 'My gears don't have syncromesh.'

81

Katie was glad that the two men got on so well. It eased some of the tension. Her second interview with the police had been just as harrowing as the first and she was ready to get away from Monaco now. Her bags had been packed and brought down to her room. The family cottage in Kent took on more and more appeal.

'When are you leaving, Don?' she asked.

'When the police let me.'

'Come and see me back in England, won't you?'

'Of course.'

'We can talk properly then.'

'You'll be most welcome, Don,' added Gerald, taking a card from his wallet and handing it over. 'We're a little off the beaten track but my wife will cook you a splendid meal.'

'Thanks, Mr Britwell.'

'Ring first for directions or you'll never find us.'

'I'll remember.'

There was a lull in the conversation. Katie took the opportunity to excuse herself and went into the bedroom. Hawker was disappointed. He had hoped for some time alone with her but Gerald Britwell was not to be shifted. The old man reminisced again.

'Montreal was your real peak,' he said wistfully.

'Yes.'

'Two gold medals. No British athlete had ever taken the 5,000 and the 10,000 at an Olympics. Then you came along. I never saw you in such form. You'd probably have won the marathon as well if you'd entered it.'

'Two finals were more than enough.'

'Then there was your wife in the long jump,' remembered Gerald. 'She lost the gold by a whisker. A wonderful competitor. I can still see that look of determination on her face as she began her run. Another medal for the Hawker collection.'

'We weren't married then,' muttered Hawker.

'Of course not. How stupid! She was Elaine Gallagher then.'

'That's right.'

'Her British long jump record still stands.'

'Yes . . .'

Gerald realized his mistake and was covered in confusion. He apologized profusely but only managed to prolong the embarrassment. Hawker tried to wave the subject away with a flick of his hand. The old man chastised himself.

'Look here, this is dreadful of me!'

'Forget it, Mr Britwell.'

'I must be going senile.'

'It was a long time ago.'

'How could I be so insensitive?' He gestured another apology. 'Put it down to the circumstances, Don. I'm afraid I'm under rather a lot of strain right now.'

'Sure.'

Gerald Britwell got up from his chair and paced around. He took a close look at his surroundings for the first time and smiled.

'You'll find our cottage a little humble after this.'

'That'll suit me fine.'

'Why do people need this kind of extravagance?'

'To boost their ego?' suggested Hawker.

'Spending money never did that for me.'

'You were an accountant.'

They traded a mild laugh then Gerald's face became serious. He glanced across at the bedroom before moving closer to Hawker.

'Katie should never have married him,' he confided.

'Mel?'

'We tried to tell her but she wouldn't listen.'

'Didn't you like him, Mr Britwell?'

'My wife did,' he said. 'He could be very charming with ladies. Phyllis liked him a lot. But neither of us trusted him.'

'Oh?'

'He was too plausible, Don. Too cocky. Too decisive for our taste.'

'I know what you mean.'

'Some of it was mindless prejudice, I daresay,' admitted Gerald. 'We're very conventional and middle class. Mel Edmunds was not exactly the son-in-law we would have chosen. Besides . . .'

'Well?'

'We liked Drew.'

'Katie's fiancé?'

'All right, he doesn't have anything like Mel's charisma. Or his wealth, come to that. But Drew is steady. He's dependable. More to the point, he worshipped Katie.'

'Didn't Mel?'

Gerald Britwell decided against a reply. Instead, he came and sat down opposite Hawker. The old man was starting to look frail.

'Thank you for all you've done.'

'I wish it could have been more.'

'Katie told me about . . . how you broke it to her. She may not seem it at the moment but she's very grateful to you, Don. If she had to find out something as appalling as that, it was the best way.'

'I hated having to do it.'

'Nobody likes to be the bearer of bad tidings,' said Gerald philosophically. 'People don't always separate the messenger from the news he brings. They blame you.'

Hawker nodded ruefully. He had been in that situation when Henri Lequesne went up to the penthouse suite. The person who had merely reported the murder was made to feel vaguely responsible for it.

'Can I ask you something, Mr Britwell?' said Hawker.

'Please do.'

'Did you ring Katie the night before last?'

'No, Don.'

'You didn't contact her at Nance Paulson's house?'

'No, I didn't.'

'Have you any idea why she went to Paris yesterday?'

'Paris?'

Gerald was plainly baffled. It was answer enough.

'Sorry,' said Hawker. 'Got my wires a bit crossed.'

'What's this about Paris?'

'Nothing, Mr Britwell. What I really wanted to ask you about was Katie herself. How will all this affect her future?'

'I wish I knew.'

'It will obviously put her out of the game for a while.'

'Yes,' agreed the other sadly. 'Such a shame! This was the best season Katie ever had. She's beaten Nance Paulson twice already and she had hopes of doing the same in the French Open. Katie's always played well at Roland Garros.' A profound sigh came. 'Then on to Wimbledon, of course. That was her dream.'

'It's still months away.'

'But will she be in the right frame of mind?'

'That's what I'm asking you, Mr Britwell.'

'It's going to take her some time to get over this,' said the old man. 'Then – with luck – she can pick up the pieces again. I just want to see her back on a tennis court again.'

'So do I.'

The bedroom door opened as they were speaking and Katie stood framed in it. She was wearing a diamond necklace of such magnificence that it made her blouse and skirt look positively dowdy. They rose to their feet to get a closer view. Katie smiled defiantly.

'It was my wedding present from Mel.'

'I know, darling,' said her father. 'It's beautiful.'

'Fantastic!' admired Hawker.

'I was going to wear it for dinner last night,' she

explained. 'Mel asked me to. I've put it on now instead.'

'You look lovely in it,' promised Gerald.

'I want to travel home like this.'

'If you wish, darling.'

'I want everyone to see how much my husband cared for me.'

She walked across to the nearest mirror to examine the necklace afresh. Her hands played with it as she made minor adjustments. Then she turned to face them. She was very calm as she delivered her bomb-shell.

'I heard what you were saying, Daddy.'

'Plenty of time to talk about that.'

'No need,' she announced. 'I've already made my decision.'

'Decision?' echoed Hawker.

'This is it. My professional career is over. I want out.'

'Katie!' cried her father in anguish.

'I'm serious,' she affirmed. 'Just look what the game has done for me. I'm not just quitting. I never want to play tennis again!'

Her certainty was quite devastating.

Robert Alexander gathered up some papers and put them in a neat pile inside his briefcase. He closed the lid, stood up, took his jacket from its hanger and slipped it on. He had a final check to make sure that he had forgotten nothing then went out. A girl looked up from a desk in the main office.

'The flight from Nice is on time, Mr Alexander.'

'Thank you, Janice.'

'Due at Heathrow in just over an hour.'

'Perfect.'

'You should make it easily in that Porsche.'

Janice had a pert charm that was wasted on Robert.

The more he ignored it, however, the more she poked it at him, widening her blue eyes, angling her face for effect and giving him an open-mouthed smile that was intended to be faintly provocative. It all passed by him. There was an indomitable brightness about the secretary that he found lowering.

'If Neil Osborne rings, confirm the lunch date for Friday.'

'Yes, Mr Alexander.'

'Chase up those files I wanted.'

'I'll do that right now.'

'Oh, yes,' he added. 'And can you give Harry Weinberger a buzz, please. Tell him that I've arranged a meeting with the All-England Club on the 28th. Eleven o'clock. Ask him to be punctual for a change.'

'Anything else, Mr Alexander?'

But Robert's attention had strayed. His gaze had wandered to the far wall of the office. A series of large colour posters had been affixed with Bluetack. Guido Barelli, Yuri Chegenyov, Nance Paulson and Lars Holmgren were all on display but it was the action shot of Mel Edmunds which mesmerized Robert. Janice swung around to see what he was looking at.

'I suppose we'll have to take that one down soon,' she remarked.

'Do that, Janice.'

'Right.'

'Put up another in its place.'

'I shall miss him,' she confessed with a nostalgic smile. 'I used to drool over Mel Edmunds. That man was so sexy.'

Robert Alexander gave her a sharp look then sailed out of the office, leaving her to wonder what she had said to annoy him. Six months of trying to engage his attention had gained her nothing more than polite detachment. Now that she had finally got beyond his unruffled calm, it was only to irritate him. She was obviously doing something wrong. Perhaps it was the open-mouthed smile.

The telephone rang on her desk. Lifting the receiver with a reflex action, she issued her standard greeting.

'International Tennis Federation. Can I help you . . .?'

For the first time since he met him, Hawker was grateful to Yves Daninos. The Chief Inspector arranged for two uniformed gendarmes to accompany Katie and her father to the courtesy limousine. Hawker went with them to discover a band of photographers lying in ambush with a support party of journalists. Katie was highly disconcerted by the media attention as she was bombarded by questions from all sides. There was even a television camera pursuing her. Hawker lent his strength to that of the policemen and helped to clear a way for her. She plunged gratefully into the car with her father.

'Goodbye, Don!' she called.

'Safe journey!' he said.

'Ring me soon.'

'I will.'

'Thank you again,' added Gerald, upset by all the tumult.

The limousine drew away with a police escort. Evidently, they were expecting more media interest at the airport. Hawker now became the centre of attention but he held up both hands to wave them away.

'No comment!'

A few of them chased him back to the hotel then gave up.

Hawker retraced the steps he had taken the previous evening. Crossing the lobby, he paused in the area where he had been accosted by Quentin Rivers then he went on to the hairdressing salon. He doubled back to the lifts and waited until the one he had used before was available. It shot him up to the top floor without stopping *en route*. Hawker came out into the corridor and strolled towards Room 1250. A large notice was pinned to the door, forbidding entry in three languages and bearing the police logo. The message was reinforced by a piece of thick tape across the architrave at chest height.

He was about to move on when he heard sounds from within. The door opened and two figures emerged, a slender young man with a dark complexion and a silver-haired gnome. As they ducked under the tape, Hawker noted the young man's expensive camera and the sketchbook carried by the other. He regarded them with a mixture of surprise and suspicion. They were patently not members of the forensic team.

The gnome's face exploded into a grin.

'Donald Hawker, I presume!'

'That's right,' conceded Hawker.

'Alain Dupont.' He gave a clammy handshake. 'And this is Dimitri, my friend and assistant.'

Hawker settled for a nod with the Greek. Their names were familiar from Nance Paulson's account of the fateful dinner party. It was a chance to corroborate facts.

'I believe you knew Mel Edmunds,' said Hawker.

'Briefly,' replied Alain. 'One night of madness then he was snatched away from me. The story of my life.'

'You had dinner with him and Katie.'

'Someone's been doing their homework!'

'Nance Paulson told me about it.'

'Then you'd better hear *our* side of the story,' insisted Alain, warming to the presence of an audience. 'Nance is a dear but she was labouring under two constraints.'

'Constraints?'

'She's a woman and she was the hostess. That made it impossible for her to see things from our standpoint. Isn't that so, Dimitri?'

'Yes,' chimed his companion.

'Let me see. How shall I begin . . .?'

Alain's narrative differed in style and emphasis. It was more of a performance than a story and he revelled in the way that he had brought out the worst in Mel Edmunds. During the dinner itself, he had cleverly goaded the American into a series of outbursts. Hawker watched him carefully but he also kept an eye on Dimitri's reactions. Alain Dupont was making light of the contempt heaped on him but Mel's barbs still hurt the young Greek. When he came to the end of his tale, the artist took a deep bow to imaginary applause.

He then looked Hawker up and down and confided a secret.

'There was a time when you were on my target list, Donald.'

'Target list?'

'There aren't all *that* many outstanding British sportsmen to immortalize on canvas. And I hadn't painted an athlete.' He grimaced. 'Then I saw you race at a televised meeting. That was that.'

'What do you mean?'

'Oh, no criticism of your ability, my love. You won the race by half a lap. But you had no *style*. You gave me nothing to work with. I wanted to paint a gazelle not a galloping cart-horse.'

'I can see why Mel hit it off with you,' noted Hawker.

Alain gave a tinny laugh but Dimitri tensed angrily.

'A pity you weren't at the dinner party, Donald,' said the artist

'Not a hope,' returned Hawker. 'Somehow I don't think I'd ever be on Croizier's guest list.'

'That's where you're wrong. Jean-Louis has a special

interest in sporting stars. Heavens above – he married one of them!'

'I don't follow.'

'You must know who he is.'

'A businessman of some sort.'

'Of some sort! Ha!' Alain let out a cackle. 'That elegant French gentleman is behind the biggest sportswear operation in Europe.'

Hawker was impressed. 'He's involved with Bellecroix?'

'He *is* Bellecroix. As the name might tell you.'

'And Nance is –'

'Sponsored by Bellecroix. He's getting there, Dimitri.'

'I never realized.'

'Jean-Louis does like to keep a low profile,' explained Alain. 'I suppose it's force of habit.'

'Habit?'

'Come on, Donald,' he chided. 'You're not *that* naïve. People who make vast amounts of money seldom do it honestly. They learn to cover their tracks. Jean-Louis is a case in point. He amassed his fortune in all kinds of shady ventures. Bellecroix is probably the only legitimate business he's run. He had to have that to capture Nance.'

'I see.'

'Don't look so shocked, dear heart,' advised Alain. 'Tolerance is our watchword on the Riviera. We live and let live. There are dozens of people like Jean-Louis Croizier in Monaco. This is where the criminals come to play at being law-abiding. Oddly enough, that's what they usually are. They do their dirty work elsewhere. Fortunately for us, they don't shit on their own doorstep.'

Hawker was beginning to wish that he *had* been at the dinner party. Jean-Louis Croizier took on a new interest for him. So did Nance Paulson. Not to mention

91

the dynamic between them. Hawker would also have liked to witness the confrontation between Alain and Mel, if only to gauge Dimitri's reactions. Though the Greek said nothing, he was part of the conversation, enjoying Alain's histrionics, glowering at Hawker's interjections, not bothering to hide a possessive streak. There was a passion in him that could easily turn to violence.

Alain Dupont made an elaborate gesture of farewell.

'You must excuse us, Donald. The muse calls.'

'Before you go,' said Hawker. 'How did you get in the room?'

'Friends in high places.'

'But why? What did you want in there?'

'Artistic licence.'

The tinny laugh went off down the corridor with Dimitri in close attendance. Hawker turned and went over to the picture window, pretending to study the panoramic view until he heard the lift arrive, open then close. Satisfied that he was alone, he pushed his way through the emergency exit.

He stood on the concrete stairwell and looked down. There were twenty steps to the fire door on the next floor and the hotel had a total of eighteen storeys. To escape the building, he had to negotiate three hundred and sixty steps and a series of fire doors. He checked his watch, got himself ready then began the descent. He was hurrying but not racing. His feet echoed on the steps and each fire door made a swishing noise as it was wrenched open. Hawker was inside one of the most lavish buildings in Monte Carlo yet he was coming down it through a cold, bare shaft.

When he reached the bottom, he lifted the release bar on the heavy steel doors and shoved them open. He was in the car-park at the rear of the premises. Surrounded by a high perimeter wall, it was quite secluded and housed a colourful mix of Ferraris,

Mercedes, Lancias, Volvos and Jaguars. A solitary Rolls Royce was on view. In the far corner, a gaping entrance led to additional spaces at a subterranean level.

Hawker remembered his watch. The journey had taken him well under two minutes. He was breathing heavily but not exhausted. If he went flat out, he estimated that he could knock ten, even fifteen, seconds off his time. Someone who was younger, lighter and faster could beat that.

He wondered if Dimitri was as fit as he looked.

Stepping back into the building, he pulled the doors after him and they clanged shut. The noise reverberated up the hollow shaft and it was accompanied by another sound, a heavy tapping. Hawker strained his ears but he could not identify it. Suddenly, all was quiet.

He tried the fire doors to his left and saw that they gave access to a corridor on the ground floor. Having decided that Mel's killer could have left by the emergency exit, he asked himself if that might also have been the mode of entry. It was a taxing climb but far more private than walking through the lobby to the lifts. He came back into the shaft and began the long ascent.

After climbing a few flights, he was really panting and he slowed down. Pushing open the next fire door, he was about to tackle another flight when his upward journey was curtailed. Something hard and powerful hit him across the back of his head with the force of a sledge-hammer. He staggered against the wall, fought to retain consciousness and stuck out his hands for protection. The second blow caught him against the forehead and knocked him senseless. As he dropped to the hard concrete, he did not even feel the sharp kick to his ribs.

What he did hear was the sound of the steel doors opening again.

In the front of his head. Blood gushed out.

He stopped worrying.

Taking care not to get too close, he trailed them all the way from Heathrow. He knew the route well, even down to the short cuts. He could happily let the Rover get out of sight without fear of losing it. The two occupants were far too bound up in their grief to pay much attention to the rear-view mirror. They had tunnel vision.

The village was over an hour's steady drive away. It was in one of the loveliest and leafiest parts of Kent and offered a kind of companionable remoteness. The cottage itself was on the edge of the village. It was not large but it had definite character. Tudor half-timbering had been carefully preserved and the mullioned windows had kept double glazing heroically at bay. The property stood towards the rear of a plot that was almost an acre in size. A well established kitchen garden gave it a post card setting.

There was also a paddock but this was for the most part obscured by a grove of sycamores. As they danced in the evening wind, it was just possible to glimpse the tennis court behind them.

Robert Alexander parked far enough away to be safe from discovery yet close enough to keep the place under surveillance. He had brought the evening papers with him to read fresh articles about the murder, and he listened to the regular news bulletins on his car radio in case one new detail might slip through. He had sandwiches, even a thermos. He had always been well prepared for things that mattered to him.

As he watched the cottage being enfolded in darkness, he tried to guess at what was happening inside. Tears, recriminations, vanished hopes. Loving parents offering solace. Old memories competing with a new disaster. Pain, loss, decay.

Would she even notice the flowers – let alone speculate who might have sent them? Had they in fact arrived? Were they a mistake? Was it too soon?

The geography of their movements was at least clear. Lights in the windows told him where they were and what they were doing. Mutual reassurance in the living room. Preparing a meal in the kitchen. Eating in the dining room. Moving back to the comfy three-piece suite with its floral pattern covers. Main light out, standard lamp on. A slow winding down after a tortured twenty-four hours.

Katie went to bed early. He followed her from the light on the landing, in the bathroom, then in her bedroom at the front of the house. She sought darkness quickly and lay there in her ruin. She would need more than sedatives that night.

There was nothing more that he could do. He had attended her in the only way that was open to him. Katie was back where she started. He would have to bide his time.

Robert switched on the ignition and eased his white Porsche back on to the main road. As he drove past the Britwell cottage, his headlights flashed across her bedroom like a soft caress.

Chapter Four

Hawker floated through a land of phantoms. Half-forgotten people and half-remembered places drifted past him in an endless stream. Then Elaine was suddenly there, laughing and waving, jumping up on her toes, strangely happy again. There was no sorrow now, only a sort of distant joy, the shared wonder of love. She beckoned him to join her, then Mel was beside her, grinning broadly, helping to draw him across. They wanted Hawker to be with them, part of them, the Elaine of old, the Mel of yesteryear, pulling him to them with an invisible rope, ready to welcome him to their special fraternity.

Closer and closer they dragged him until he could almost touch them. Elaine called, Mel urged, both heaved on the rope with all their might. Hawker let go and dived forward but his hands only brushed Elaine's as he fell. Her voice sighed through oblivion after him.

They were gone for good as the steel doors were slammed shut on his forehead. The spurting blood now swirled around inside his skull. Strong men with large pickaxes waded through the morass and struck at solid steel. Each pounding blow threatening to split his head apart. Hawker closed his eyes tight against the juddering agony but it would not go away. When he opened them, there was a chink of light between the steel doors.

The first person he saw through the slit was Chabrier.

'*Bonsoir, M'sieur . . .*'

Hawker closed his eyes once more and searched for Elaine but she had vanished now. He could still feel the touch of her hand against his and he listened in the booming darkness for the sound of her call.

'You are a lucky man, M'sieur Hawker.'

The doors had parted much wider now. When he raised an eyelid to peep between them, he saw another phantom leaning over him.

'How do you feel now?'

Yves Daninos was standing by his bedside with concern.

'Where am I?' croaked Hawker.

'In hospital. Do not try to move.'

'Hospital!'

The shock made Hawker ignore the advice. When he struggled to sit up, he found that his chest was encased in concrete and the steel doors banged to and fro on his forehead. A nurse moved in to help him, adjusting the pillows behind him, easing his pain, stilling his resistance. She held a plastic cup to his lips and water trickled down his dry, constricted throat. The nurse stepped back but stayed in the room. He could see her blurred outline behind the looming faces of the two policemen.

'What happened?' he whispered.

'You tell us,' said Daninos.

'How did I get here?'

'You were found by a security man at the hotel,' explained the other. 'On the staircase of the emergency exit. That is why you are lucky, M'sieur. He got to you before you had lost much blood. There was a gash in your head. They have put stitches in. You have other marks on your face, I'm afraid, and you do not look very pretty.'

Raoul Chabrier came perilously close to a smile.

'What about my . . .?' Hawker's hand went to his chest.

'You must have ribs of iron, M'sieur,' congratulated Daninos. 'Heavy bruising but nothing cracked. You will be fine in the morning. They can release you from hospital.'

Morbid fear made him try to sit up again.

'I can't stay here!' he protested.

'Relax, M'sieur.'

'You've no right to keep me.'

'The doctor recommends it.'

'I want to get out.'

A savage pain in his head slowed him down. The nurse came over again and made him more comfortable. He was now in a sitting position and the agony was slowly fading. The nurse gave him another drink, had a few words with Daninos, then left the room. Four bare walls and two policemen. Hawker felt trapped. Helpless. At their mercy.

'How are you now, M'sieur?' asked Daninos.

'Terrific!' he said with heavy sarcasm.

'You are getting your sense of humour back. Good.'

'Shall I tell you a few jokes?'

'I think you have told us enough of those already, M'sieur.'

'Look, I want to get out of this place.'

'Don't you like it?'

'No.'

'But it is much better than that little room at your hotel,' said the Chief Inspector persuasively. 'It is clean, comfortable and they wait on you hand and foot. You have had a bad time but now we have good news for you.'

'Being locked in here?'

'Only for one night, M'sieur. Besides, you are not being restrained. If you had the strength to walk out, you could discharge yourself at any time. You are a free man.'

'So what's this good news?' asked Hawker suspiciously.

'You may go home.'

'To England?'

'There is a flight at eleven in the morning,' said Daninos. 'Raoul has made a reservation for you. We will arrange transport to the airport.'

'Thanks.'

'You see? We can be a help to you, M'sieur.'

'What's the catch?'

'You must be a help to us.'

'Ah.'

'Is it so difficult?'

'Try me.'

'Let us deal with this attack on you first.'

'Attack?' Hawker put up a tentative hand to feel his head. 'Is that what it was, Chief Inspector.'

'We are in for more trouble, Raoul,' warned Daninos.

Chabrier grunted and took out his notebook.

'Help us to help *you*, M'sieur,' he suggested.

'How?'

'To begin with,' said Daninos, 'tell us what you were doing in the emergency exit at the Hotel Brassard.'

'Trying to find a way out.'

'M'sieur Hawker,' warned the Chief Inspector. 'We can always postpone this interview until the morning. It is very late now and we are both ready to go home to our beds. Would you like Raoul to cancel your flight so that you can stay with us a little longer?'

'No,' said Hawker.

'So what were you doing?'

'Wondering if that's how the killer got away.'

'*We* are the detectives, M'sieur.'

'I was curious, that's all.'

99

'So you went down the steps.'

'I'll take the lift next time.'

'What happened?'

'I don't know, Chief Inspector. I must have slipped.'

Daninos sighed and Chabrier looked quite disgusted. They had a wordless conference then the senior man turned back to the bed. His patience was becoming ragged at the edges.

'One more time,' he said. 'Just one. That is all. Before you answer, consider this. Would a trained athlete like yourself trip on concrete steps? Would you be facing *up* the staircase if you had fallen downwards? And if you got that gash when you fell forward, how did you get the lump on the back of your head and the bruising on the side of your ribs?' He smiled wearily. 'Why not tell us the truth?'

'I would if I knew what it was,' admitted Hawker. 'All I can remember is that I got to the bottom of the steps, opened the doors to the car-park, closed them again then started to climb. When I'd got up three or four flights, I went through this door and something hit me from behind. The lights went out. That's it, honestly.'

'You have no idea who it was?'

'None at all.'

He did but he was holding the information back. Hawker liked to fight his own battles. He did not want the police to exact revenge on his behalf. There would be no personal satisfaction in that.

'Let us go back to the start of your day,' suggested Daninos.

'Why?'

'Because we need you to fill in the blanks.'

Chabrier flipped back to an earlier page in his notebook.

He read out his jottings in a flat monotone, making an imperfect translation as he went along. It was all there. Hawker's run, shower, meagre breakfast and telephone calls. The journalist was outraged.

'You've been *tailing* me!

'No, M'sieur,' said Chabrier. 'We ask at the hotel, that is all.'

'It saves manpower,' added Daninos cheerily. 'The hotel keeps a record of all the numbers it dials and the length of each call. It was very convenient for us.'

Hawker was still seething. 'Why not go the whole hog and bug the phone? Why not instal a two-way mirror in my room?'

'I will come to that,' said Daninos.

'You two certainly know how to make tourists feel welcome!'

'Let's go through those calls, shall we?' suggested the Chief Inspector blithely. 'Why did you ring the Hotel Brassard?'

'To see how Katie was.'

'And?'

'She asked me to call round later. Meet her father.'

'Good. A straight answer at last.'

'Then I gave the airport a bell.'

'We know. They were helpful to you?'

'Very.'

'Thank Raoul for that. He warned them in advance that you would wish to alter your flight plans. They were told to oblige.'

'Oh. I see.'

'Who is Eric Fretton?'

'The editor of my magazine,' said Hawker. 'I rang to tell him I couldn't fulfil a commitment at Wembley tonight. Thanks to you. I also asked him for some legal advice.'

'About what, M'sieur?'

'Police harassment!'

Chabrier actually laughed then commuted the laugh to a grin. His colleague made a wry aside to him then resumed his questioning.

'You then rang the home of Monsieur Croizier.'

'To speak to his wife. Nance Paulson.'

'Why?'

'Because I'm a journalist, that's why,' argued Hawker, putting up a smokescreen. 'Been trying to interview Nance for months. Since one story packed up on me, I wanted to get another. My editor turns nasty if I go back empty-handed.'

'That brings us to Guido Barelli.'

'Couldn't get through to him.'

'The call lasted over two minutes.'

'His wife was telling me why he had gone to Rome.'

'Is that all she was telling you?'

'What?'

'Did she share any reminiscences about Monsieur Edmunds?'

'I wanted her husband,' said Hawker irritably. 'For a quote. First thing I have to do when I get home is to write an obit for Mel. I want quotes from some of the top players.'

'Even the ones whose wives have known Monsieur Edmunds?' Daninos raised a cynical eyebrow. 'We both know the sort of thing that Barelli would say. Your magazine would not be able to print it. You rang to speak to Lia. What man would not like to do that?'

He glanced at Chabrier who took a sheet of paper from his inside pocket and unfolded it. Daninos studied the patient once more.

'Feeling any better now?'

'No.'

'This will not take long.'

'M'sieur,' said Chabrier, referring to the typed page, 'this is a copy of the statement you gave us yesterday at the Hotel Brassard.'

'So?'

'We do not think it is accurate.'

'Let me give you an example,' said Daninos

mischievously. 'You said that you left the final at the Country Club and went back to your hotel with Mademoiselle Eriksson.'

'That was true!' insisted Hawker.

'Half-true,' said Chabrier.

'Yes,' agreed Daninos. 'You forgot to mention to us that you and the young lady made love.'

'Hey, now come on!' yelled Hawker.

'Why deny it?' asked Daninos. 'She does not.'

'You've *spoken* to Christina?'

'Of course. To check your story. The hotel porter gave us the number in Hamburg.' Daninos smiled. 'She sounded very nice. When I asked her what you did at the hotel, she giggled. That is what I meant about the two-way mirror, M'sieur. We do not need one when we have a lovely young lady to tell us what we wish to know.'

Hawker was barely managing to contain his fury. The two men had the advantage over him and they were pressing it home. Daninos clicked his fingers and Chabrier read out the typed statement in his monotone. Hawker could hear how disjointed and unconvincing it sounded. When it was all over, Daninos beamed at him.

'Fill in the blanks.'

'What blanks?'

'Go through it all again. *Slowly.*'

'You have such a winning bedside manner,' observed Hawker tartly.

'Start with the final.'

'I am ready, M'sieur,' said the man with the notebook.

'Give us detail,' ordered Daninos. 'And colour.'

Hawker did his best to ignore the kettle drums that were being played inside his brain. He went through his story again, giving it more texture, yielding more hard fact. He hinted that the marriage between Mel

103

and Katie was under strain and talked about her unexplained absence from the early part of the final. He even mentioned the two names at the top of his private list of suspects.

Yuri Chegenyov and Guido Barelli.

'Chegenyov?' said Daninos with light mockery. 'A KGB plot?'

'Professional jealousy.'

'And Barelli?'

'Another kind of jealousy.'

'Who else?'

'I don't know yet.'

He did not divulge the other names on his list. Nor did he tell them about the address book. That was *his* clue and it would take him on a route that they could not follow.

Daninos probed and pressurized for the best part of an hour then settled for what he had got. Hawker tried to get some reciprocal facts from him.

'Have you established the time of death?'

'Yes, M'sieur.'

'Is it a state secret?'

'No. He was killed not long before you found him.'

'What about the murder weapon?'

'That is confidential information.'

'Please, Chief Inspector. Just tell me this. Was it that ashtray?'

Daninos scrutinized him as if weighing something up.

'No, M'sieur,' he finally admitted. 'The murder weapon is unknown.'

'There must've been particles in the wound.'

'Possibly.'

'What were they?' asked Hawker. 'Metal? Wood? Stone?'

'Stop trying to do our job for us,' cautioned Daninos. 'Unless you want to finish up like Monsieur Edmunds.'

'What do you mean?'

'As I said before, you are a lucky man.'

'I feel it!' groaned Hawker.

'Your assailant had you down,' Daninos pointed out. 'He could very easily have finished you off.'

'Then why didn't he?'

'Because this was just a warning. Take it.'

Hawker endured pain to produce a crooked smile.

'I'll think about it.'

Daninos clasped his hands behind his back and strutted around the bed like a giant stork about to peck for food. He brought his face to within inches of Hawker's.

'We have been learning things about you, M'sieur.'

'I bet that was fun.'

'The incident with the gold medals was only part of it.'

'Been reading my crime dossier?'

'A rebel, that's what he is, Raoul.'

'*Oui, M'sieur l'Inspecteur Principal.*'

'Constant battles with authority.'

'Standing up for my rights, that's all,' argued Hawker.

'*Il cherche les ennuis,*' said Chabrier.

'*Exactement, Raoul. Il est casse-pieds.*'

'*Un agitateur.*'

'*Il se promène toujours avec le code sous le bras.*'

'Mind insulting me in my own language?' complained Hawker.

'Keep out of our way,' said Daninos.

'My pleasure!'

'This is not your case.'

'Matter of opinion.'

'Goodbye, M'sieur!'

Daninos spun on his heel and led the way out. Hawker felt an immediate sense of release. He examined the bandaging around his chest and investigated the ache in his legs. Nothing was broken. On one side of the room was a small washbasin with a mirror above it. Hawker made an enormous effort to get out of bed, lowering his feet gingerly to the floor and fighting off the urge to keel straight over. His head now felt as if a huge ball-bearing was rolling around inside it.

Moving with tiny steps, he went across the room until he could see himself in the mirror. It had been a grievous mistake.

'Fuck!'

The Kingzett Tennis Centre was a vast modern complex which sought to cater for all levels of the sport. It had a dozen outdoor courts, six indoor courts and an exhibition court which could seat five hundred spectators and which had been used for national indoor championships. A gymnasium and leisure pool were additional attractions and there was ample chalet accommodation for any groups wishing to come on one of the coaching courses. Set in rolling parkland in Hampshire, the centre had proved itself a success in its five year existence. Much of that success could be attributed to its director.

'Do you know when *I* will be able to speak to her?'

'I'm afraid not.'

'How is she, Mr Britwell?'

'Still very groggy.'

'How long will she be in England?'

'Hard to say.'

'I don't suppose she's had time to make any plans?'

'No, Drew,' said Gerald Britwell, wheezing slightly. 'Things are in a state of flux at the moment. We're just taking each day as it comes.'

'Of course.'

'We don't even know when the funeral will be yet.'

'What have the police said?'

'Very little.' Gerald's emphysema made him wheeze again. 'They're holding on to the body for further post-mortem examination. As soon as the release is signed, Mel will be flown home.'

'New York?' asked Drew.

'Westport, Connecticut. His parents have a house there. Mel will be buried in the local cemetery.'

Drew Grant could hear the old man's laboured breathing at the other end of the line. The conversation was evidently a trial for him.

'I'd better let you go now,' volunteered Drew.

'Thanks for calling.'

'Give Katie my love.'

'Surely.'

'She knows where to find me if . . .' He abandoned the faint hope. 'Just tell her I'm thinking of her. Goodbye, Mr Britwell.'

'Cheerio, Drew.'

The receiver was put down at the Kingzett Tennis Centre.

Drew Grant was a tall, rangy individual in his early thirties. The freckles on his boyish face were set off by a shock of red hair. Though born in London, he was of Scots parentage and had a light but discernible Edinburgh accent. Tennis was the ruling passion in his life. A brilliant junior, he made an immediate impact on the senior game and lifted British hearts by his performances in Davis Cup matches. Then cartilege trouble brought his playing career to a premature end. Determined to stay in the game, he set out on the path that was to lead to the Kingzett Tennis Centre.

As he gazed out now through the window of his office, he could see all the outside courts in use. It was an inspiring sight and it had never failed to thrill him to the core. Until today. A controversial choice as director of the centre, he had brought flair, commitment and enthusiasm to his job, the net result of which was a flourishing business. He was entitled to feel proud of his achievement but he could not muster the slightest interest in it at the moment.

When he looked at the twelve courts, he could see Katie Britwell playing on each one of them. When he gazed across at the leisure pool, he could see the place where he proposed to her. And when his eyes travelled to the exhibition court, where he and Katie had had some fine matches together, he saw the place where she had finally agreed to marry him. The burgeoning success of the Kingzett Tennis Centre was fringed with personal sorrow.

Drew turned away from the window and wandered aimlessly around the office. Unable to speak to Katie directly, he was desperate to open some lines of communication. Her parents were on his side but they were not a decisive factor. The sudden marriage to Mel Edmunds proved that. Drew would have to find some other means of getting in touch.

A name popped into his mind and he liked the sound of it.

He grabbed the telephone and rang Directory Enquiries.

Running a monthly sports magazine was a costly and onerous business. The budget would not stretch to a suite of modern offices or a large permanent staff. So the magazine operated out of two rooms above a wine bar near Wandsworth Common. In times of stress – on average, once a week – editorial decisions were made in the wine bar itself. A judicious glass of Sauternes helped the creative juices to flow.

Eric Fretton was a small, round, dyspeptic man with a roly-poly face and a mistaken loyalty to denim. In jeans, waistcoat and check shirt, he looked like a superannuated hippie. A fondness for badges turned his chest into a paradise of graffiti. He was his own wall. Thirty years in journalism had given him ulcers, enemies and an instinct for what would work. Rewards of the heart only partially atoned for the lack of a prestige salary.

Eric was not a man to conceal his feelings.

'Bloody hell!'

'Hi, Eric!'

'You look like something out of a bad horror movie.'

'Thanks.'

'I have warned you about picking up rough women.'

'Just give me a cup of coffee and stop staring at me.'

Don Hawker perched on the edge of the desk in the editor's cramped office. The two chairs were piled high with back copies of the magazine. The walls were a mass of sports posters and comic slogans and printing schedules. Eric Fretton was sitting in the middle of a sea of paper. He swam into a standing position.

'Is that really *you*, Hawker?'

'No!'

'Christ Al-bloody-mighty!'

'Eric . . .'

'Bugger me with a broom handle!'

'Don't keep on. It hurts enough as it is.'

'Whatever happened?'

'I'll tell you over coffee.'

'Follow the leader.'

Eric bustled through into what had once been the front bedroom of the house. Three desks had been crammed in along with filing cabinets, steel cupboards, copious shelving and a mammoth copying machine. The percolator was bubbling happily in a corner. Eric put two plastic cups on top of a heavily-laden trolley and poured coffee into them. While they spoke, he automatically added milk to one and three heaped spoonfuls of sugar to the other.

'Where is everybody?' said Hawker, looking around.

'Tony is at the printer's, Geoff is out on a story and you can guess where the lovely Zoe is.' He pulled a face. 'Gone home early because she's having a bad period. Ever since that girl joined us, *we've* been having a bad period. If she didn't have such an amazing pair of knockers, I'd give her the elbow.'

'Zoe is very efficient.'

'Oh, sure. When she's here.'

'She's as useful as Tony.'

'But Tony doesn't flake out on me once a month.' He handed the sugarless coffee to Hawker. 'Anyway, probably just as well our Zoe isn't here. If she saw you like that, she'd have Siamese kittens.'

'I've stopped looking in mirrors,' confessed Hawker.

'How many have you cracked?'

They settled into chairs. Hawker had been well enough to travel home from Monte Carlo but he was still in discomfort. His legs hurt, his head throbbed and the side of his ribs was one long dull ache. A plaster had been stuck across his forehead to hide the stitches but the colourful bruising spilled out beyond its edges. There were ugly abrasions on his cheeks and one eye was spectacularly black.

Eric found him an object of continuing fascination.

'You know, I've seen men go three rounds with Mike Tyson and come out in better shape than you. What hit you? A double-decker bus?'

'Not exactly.'

'Tell me all.'

Hawker gave him an edited version of the events on a concrete staircase. The editor chipped in with his brand of cruel sympathy and sipped noisily at his coffee. One question dominated.

'Who did it?'

'Tell you when I find him.'

'You know?'

'Think so.'

'Same man who bumped off Mel Edmunds?'

'Could be.'

'Hey, you go easy,' warned the editor. 'We can't afford danger money. Leave the rough stuff to the coppers.'

'It's my story, Eric. I owe it to Katie.'

'As long as the mag reaps the benefit.'

'It will. Just bear with me. Meanwhile, I'll keep up with the routine stuff so that you're not short of copy.' He tasted his coffee. 'Any feedback on this month's edition?'

'Plenty!' moaned the editor.

'Problems?'

'Mega-problems.'

'Why?'

'Your article on the role of the football manager.'

'You told me to spice it up.'

'Oh, you did that okay,' agreed Fretton. 'The shit has been hitting the fan at a rate of knots. There may be libel suits.'

'All good publicity.'

'Spare me the cheery platitudes.' The telephone rang in his office. 'Answer that, will you? If it's Val, tell her I had to go out.'

'Where?'

'Who cares?'

'Don't you want to speak to your wife?'

'Just answer the bloody thing!'

Hawker smiled and went through into the smaller office to do the chore. Eric Fretton stiffened when he heard his colleague's affable treachery coming through the door.

'Yes, Val. He's right here. Hold on . . .'

'Hawker, you're fired!' howled Eric.

'He's dying to talk to you, Val.'

'Bastard!'

The editor stormed into his office to be met with a grin.

'It's Nev,' said Hawker.

'Stop pissing about.' Eric chuckled with relief and snatched the receiver from him. 'Nev? Hello, baby. How's it all going . . .?'

Hawker left him to it and came back into the other room. After another sip of coffee, he wandered across to the packed shelves to search for a book. The current edition of *World of Tennis* was jammed in between a cricketing autobiography and a rugby union encyclopaedia.

Hawker pulled the volume out. Published in association with the International Tennis Federation, it had the distinctive logo on the front cover – a green tennis ball franked with the initials ITF. Hawker was more interested in the colour picture above it. As befitted the number one player, Mel Edmunds had pride of place. Caked with sweat and high on adrenalin, he was about to play a backhand volley at some unseen opponent. The sight of the young American in full flow gave Hawker a twinge of deep regret.

He leafed through the pages. Nance Paulson was praised as the leading women's player and there were a number of photographs of her, all featuring Bellecroix sportswear. Chegenyov, Barelli, Holmgren and all the other stars of the circuit had their moment in black and white. Hawker was not concerned with the men. He was hunting three names he had seen in someone's address book.

The action shot of Patti Baff was taken in the glare of the Melbourne sunshine. Short, dark but exceptionally shapely, the girl had definite outdoor charm and it was easy to see why Mel had been tempted, but Patti Baff was not a woman to hold his interest for long. Nor would she have wanted to do so. She liked to run with the pack.

Hawker next came to a photograph of Ingrid Bellinghausen, the long, lovely Californian blonde with the vestiges of her Germanic background still visible. Ingrid had the standard good looks that would appeal to most men but there was no special quality about her. Hawker wondered what Mel had found in her that made it important enough for him to keep track of her around the States.

Jody Beecher was the least photogenic of them. Slim and slight, she had a college girl look to her. The pigtails were practical but not flattering. Pictured at full stretch on the baseline, she had a feline grace but nothing like the presence of the other two players. There was an incidental bonus for Hawker. Beneath Jody Beecher was the name of the photographer — C. Erikkson. Even such a stray encounter with Christina was heartening. He thought of Monte Carlo.

Turning to the reference section in the book, he consulted the biographies of the three players. Patti Baff had risen as high as number four in the world rankings but she had slipped back to sixteenth position in the previous season. She was still a fine player on her day but the best of her tennis was now probably behind her. Ingrid Bellinghausen, by contrast, had made steady improvement over the years to get into the top ten. Consistency was her hallmark.

Jody Beecher was a teenage sensation. She reached the semi-finals in her first Wimbledon when she was only sixteen. Looking at her career record, Hawker wondered if the girl did anything else but play tennis. She was amassing a formidable list of successes. Still only nineteen, she had been ranked fifth in the previous season. Hawker noted that Jody Beecher was also a very talented doubles player.

As he put the book back on the shelf, he reflected on

the sort of man Mel Edmunds must have been – a compulsive lecher in search of a new conquest? Patti Baff, Ingrid Bellinghausen and Jody Beecher were such differing characters. A man would have to be fairly undiscriminating to pursue all three with equal vigour. Patti for a brief affair, maybe. Jody for no more than a night, surely. Only Ingrid might have lasted any length of time.

All three paled beside Lia Barelli.

Eric Fretton came waddling out of his office in mild despair.

'Why did I appoint that man as circulation manager?'

'Neville?'

'Whenever he talks to me, he *stops* my circulation. I can feel the blood congealing in my veins. It's not good for me.'

'Take more exercise,' urged Hawker.

'Maybe I should go on a climbing tour of Zoe's tits.'

'It's the wrong time of the month.'

'Bound to be a disaster, anyway.'

'Why?'

'As I was coming around the north face of the right one, it would be just my luck to meet Tony going the other way.'

'She's a nice girl,' said Hawker. 'Don't mock her.'

'I adore the kid,' asserted Eric. 'Office life wouldn't be the same without Zoe. What other secretary carries two of the Seven Wonders of the World around with her?'

'Can we talk about work for a minute?'

'Please! I've got lots of things lined up for you, Hawker. If you can fit them into your busy schedule of murder, sex and violence.' He suddenly slapped his forehead hard. 'Oops! Sorry!'

'What's up?'

114

'Went straight out of my mind. You had an urgent phone call.'

'Katie Britwell?' he said hopefully.

'No, it was a bloke.' He groped around for the name.

'Not Daninos or Chabrier, was it?'

'He was English. Used to play tennis. Tip of my tongue.'

'Drew Grant?'

'That's him! How did you guess?'

'What did he want?'

'You. On the blower. Pronto.'

Yuri Chegenyov usually became impatient with his practice partners. If they did not measure up to his exacting standards, he either abused them or tried to give them a coaching lesson.

'Turn your body!' he called. 'Turn your body into the shot!'

'Ja!'

'That's it! Turn!'

He played the ball to his opponent's forehand a few times and the young German followed his advice. Chegenyov soon found something else to criticize.

'Drive it hard!' he insisted.

'Ja!'

'Stay down low on your shots! Stay low!'

Big, strong and willing, the German tried to do as he was told, keeping the ball in play as the Russian clipped it effortlessly across the net to him. More advice came.

'Punch the volley! Punch the volley!'

'I will.'

'Come on – harder!'

But the German's power was greater than his control. When he put more force into his volleying, the ball smacked into the net. Chegenyov had had enough. After thanking the young man for the practice session, he walked off court and reached for his towel.

They were in Hamburg on the morning before the Russian was due to play Ivan Bacic, the left-handed Yugoslavian. Alex had found him a left-handed practice partner but Chegenyov had tired of him very quickly. He would wait until Alex himself came back then they could play together.

One of the photographers drifted past the court.

'Hi, there,' she said.

'Hello.'

'Enjoyed your match against Steiner yesterday.'

'Thank you.' He grinned. 'Hey, you want a picture?'

'Why not?'

He had noticed Christina Erikkson at other tournaments. She was a rare female in what was largely a male preserve, part of the itinerant army of sports photographers that trailed the big events around the world. A fair-haired Scandinavian with a friendly smile, she favoured loose-fitting clothes that went with her easy manner. Chegenyov was drawn to her at once. She had a relaxed frankness he did not often find in Russian girls. He wished that he had more of the bright smalltalk that the other players seemed to turn on when there was female interest around.

Christina focused the smaller of her two cameras.

'Smile, please,' she asked.

'How's this?' He beamed ferociously.

'Too much.'

'Better?' he said, looking more serious.

'In between the two.'

He put his hands on his hips and experimented with a muted grin. Christina took a few shots of him then nodded in gratitude.

'That was great.'

'Do I get a copy, please?' he asked.

'If you like.'

'I do.' He moved across to her. 'I am Yuri.'

116

'We all know that,' she said with candid admiration.

'And you?'

'Christina Erikkson.'

'Hello, Christina.'

They shook hands and he pressed her fingers tightly.

'Well, okay,' she said, pulling away. 'See you around.'

'Don't forget my photo.'

'Let you have a copy tomorrow.'

Now that he could see her close to, he liked her even more. He cursed his awkwardness and inexperience. Other players would have got much further in less time. Guido Barelli needed only sixty seconds and a few honeyed phrases. Mel Edmunds could do it all with a glance.

'There is a favour I wish to ask,' he said.

'Ask away.'

'When the tournament is over . . .'

His request died on his lips. Alex Kutsk was hurrying towards them. Wearing a track suit over his tennis strip, Alex did not seem at all pleased to spot the pair of them together. Chegenyov introduced Christina and there were a few pleasantries, then she walked off.

Alex waited until she was out of earshot.

'Who was that?' he questioned.

'Nobody. Just a friend.'

'You don't have time for friends, Yuri.'

'We were only chatting.'

'She's a distraction. Women will ruin your tennis. Ignore them.' He gazed after Christina. 'Maybe I should have a word with her.'

'No, Alex. Don't do that, please.'

His coach was too fond of frightening women away from the player. Chegenyov thought of half a dozen blighted romances that could be laid at Alex's door. This time it would be different. He would court his new friend by stealth. An assignation with Christina would be fixed for the end of the week.

But even that young hope was strangled at birth.

'I have heard from Moscow,' announced Alex grimly.

'And?'

'They want you back for an exhibition match with Zagoretski.'

'When?'

'As soon as the tournament is over.'

'No,' protested Chegenyov.

'There is a flight to Moscow the same evening.'

'But I don't want to play Zagoretski.'

'We have no choice in the matter, Comrade.'

'Suppose I don't go?' challenged the other.

Alex gave him a basilisk stare and spoke with gruff menace.

'Even you are not that stupid, Yuri.'

Chegenyov grounded his teeth in frustration then capitulated with a nod. It was always the same. Mother Russia kept her children tied to her apron strings. His disillusion deepened still further.

They had met briefly once before. Drew Grant escorted Katie Britwell to a sporting charity and they had bumped into Hawker. Even on such fleeting acquaintance, the journalist had formed a good impression of Drew. The respect was mutual.

'Thanks for seeing me at such short notice, Don.'

'Sorry to haul you up to London.'

'No problem.'

'Feel a bit awkward in public,' explained Hawker. 'People stare at me as if I'm something from outer space.'

'I'll try not to do the same.'

They were sitting in Hawker's flat in Fulham. It was small but snug and had an amiable clutter of sporting

118

memorabilia. The absence of a female touch was very noticeable. Drew Grant could not miss the large photograph of Elaine that stood on the colour television. He knew the story and it caused him a pang.

A glass of beer apiece got them through the preliminaries.

'Let's get down to it, shall we?' suggested Hawker.

'Please.'

'You want to know about Katie?'

'Tell me everything.'

Hawker launched into his account once more, noting how familiar it had become to him and observing how he tailored it to suit each listener. All that Drew Grant was interested in was Katie. He was less concerned with the murder itself than with its effect on her. Sitting on the edge of his chair, he plied Hawker with questions, grateful for the tiniest detail about his former fiancée.

Drew finished the beer in his glass and looked tentative.

'Did Katie ever mention me?' he wondered.

'No,' said Hawker.

'Not even a passing reference?'

'Nothing.'

It was the truth but it obviously wounded Drew. He clasped his hands tightly then looked down to examine them. After a few moments, he raised his eyes again. They were full of a distant pain.

'What will she do now, Don?'

'I don't know.'

'Her father said that she had no definite plans.'

'That's not quite true.'

'Oh?'

'She's quitting.'

'*What*!' Drew was aghast.

'That's what she told us in Monte Carlo,' added Hawker sadly. 'And it wasn't said in the heat of the moment either. Katie wants to turn her back on tennis completely.'

'But that's madness!'

'She seemed pretty certain about her decision.'

'We can't let her do that!' wailed Drew.

'How can we stop her?'

'After all it's cost me! She *mustn't*!'

Drew Grant went mildly berserk. Leaping to his feet, he stalked around the room, ranting away to himself, slapping the table with his hand, contorting his features into a mask of pure rage. He ignored Hawker completely. The latter was amazed at such behaviour from an apparently calm and rational man. Drew soon came to his senses and exerted control. He sat down quickly in his armchair.

'Hey, look. I'm sorry.'

'Have another drink.'

'I shouldn't have flipped like that.'

'Forget it.'

The second beer helped to soothe his guest. Hawker was glad when the meeting was arranged. He was quite willing to tell Drew about Katie because he anticipated valuable information in return. Drew had been close to her for a very long time and he was completely enmeshed in the tennis scene. Hawker went fishing.

'You coached Katie at the start, didn't you?'

'I discovered her, Don,' said the other simply. 'She was a natural but you still have to put the work in. I was the one who pushed her into a tennis scholarship in the States. That's what did the trick.'

'Made in Britain. Assembled in America.'

'Just about. I saw her whenever I could and we kept in touch by mail.' He shrugged. 'That's how it started, really.'

'What?'

'Our romance – if that's what you can call it.' Drew was bitter. 'We'd been corresponding for ages. Then the letters got more personal. We began to see how much we meant to each other.' The bitterness became more pronounced. 'At least, that's what I persuaded myself.'

'In what way?'

'Oh, I suppose there's a sexual element in all coach-player relationships. Where it's a male-female one, anyway. You begin as a sort of father figure. Then you become a best friend. Then it goes on beyond that.' He gave a wry chuckle. 'You have the illusion of being in control. Of calling all the shots.'

'How long were you and Katie engaged?'

'Best part of a year.'

'Had you set a date?'

'Twice,' explained Drew. 'Katie changed her mind both times. I should have seen the writing on the wall then.' He took a long drink from his glass. 'I was kidding myself, Don. I was never really the man for Katie Britwell. She's a high-flier now. She's outgrown me.'

'When did it break up?' asked Hawker gently.

'Last summer. But the cracks had been there for ages.'

'Too much time apart?'

'That was one factor.'

'What else?'

'Him, mainly.' Drew's face hardened. 'He just wouldn't leave her alone. Wherever she was, it was the same story – flowers, phone calls, letters, incessant badgering. He just kept on and on at her. I warned him but that still didn't stop him. He persecuted Katie. You can see why she got into such a state.'

'I didn't realize Mel had chased her like that.'

'I'm not talking about Mel. This was Alexander.'

'Who?'

'Robert Alexander. From the ITF.'

*

121

The Porsche inched its way through the thick traffic of Kensington then turned down a side-road and gathered speed. Wending its way past a series of parked vehicles, it went around another corner and accelerated slightly, only to slow down again when it came to an imposing but tastefully designed block of flats. Robert Alexander drove in through the entrance and brought the Porsche to a halt in front of a metal plate that bore his name. All the other cars on the forecourt were in their appointed places as well. Order pleased him.

Carrying his briefcase, he went up to his flat and let himself in. His first task was to scour the evening papers but they had scant interest for him. The murder of Mel Edmunds was a fading news item. It merited no more than a few lines and produced no new photographs of Katie Britwell. The police as yet had nothing dramatic to report but their enquiries had now spread beyond the boundaries of Monaco.

Robert put the paper aside and crossed to his desk. Depressing a switch on the answerphone, he rewound the tape then played it back to himself. There were a few messages from friends and then his mother's voice issued forth, filling the room with its rounded vowels, its Home Counties snobbery and its perfect enunciation.

'Hello, darling. I expected you back earlier than this. Why do I always miss you? Just to say that I'll be going down to Brighton for the weekend to stay with the Callards. Actually, you were invited as well but I explained to them how fiendishly busy you always are. Let's talk when I get back, shall we? Oh, yes, and thank you so much for the charming post card. How *was* Paris . . .?

Lia Barelli was putting the last few items into her suitcase when he came into the bedroom. Keeping her back to him, she tensed all over and pursed her lips in exasperation. Guido sauntered over to her.

'Lia,' he purred.

'Go away!'

'Lia, my angel . . .'

'Don't touch me!'

Her snarl made his hands freeze in mid-air only inches from her shoulders. Guido backed away a few paces. She was in one of her moods and he had to tread warily. He watched her finish her packing, then close the lid of her suitcase.

'What time do you arrive in Brussels?' he asked.

'That's my business.'

'Where will you be staying?'

'Never mind!' she snapped.

'But I like to know where you are, my love.'

She swung round with eyes that were pools of liquid fire.

'Yes, Guido. You do, don't you?'

'What do you mean?'

'Rome.'

'I was visiting Mama.'

'While I was still here.'

'She is a sick woman. A son must care for his mother.'

'You disgust me!'

'Why?'

'Just leave me alone!'

'But I thought it was better now, my sweet,' he said softly, trying to smother her anger beneath a pillow of tender words. 'We have a whole new future together. All those promises we made to each other. They can come true now, Lia. We can put the past behind us and forget it ever happened.' He stepped towards her. 'I love you.'

'Go back to Rome!' she yelled.

'But I do, my angel. I love you more than ever.'

123

'Tell that to your whore! She might believe you!'

Lia tried to walk past him but he grabbed her wrist as his temper flared. She struggled wildly to get free.

'Let go of me, Guido!'

'Who do you think you are?' he growled.

'Let go!'

She sank her teeth into his hand. Though he howled in pain, he did not release her. He pulled her roughly to him and she squirmed and kicked then he flung her backwards on the bed. Panting freely, she looked up at him with undisguised loathing. He rubbed his injured wrist and glowered at her.

'She is not a whore,' he insisted.

'Get out!'

'She is an actress!'

'So you *were* with her in Rome.'

'Can you blame me when this is what I get at home?'

'You are nothing but filth!' she said with utter disdain.

'And what are you – you tramp!'

'Shut your mouth!'

'I thought it would be different when he got married but it wasn't. You were still his. Weren't you?' He swung his foot at the bed. 'Weren't you!'

'Don't you dare mention him, Guido!' she warned.

'Why not?' he goaded. 'I had *my* whore. Mel Edmunds had *his*!'

'No!' she cried.

'I wish you were dead along with him.'

Lia Barelli sat up on the bed and mustered all her dignity.

'Mel was worth ten of you, Guido!'

The insult wounded him to the quick. Letting out a yell of rage, he advanced on her to wreak revenge but he was checked at the very last second. Strong knuckles rapped on the other side of the door.

Vincente let them know he had heard everything.

'The car is waiting, signora,' he said artlessly. 'Shall I take your suitcase down now?'

Katie was still in the bath when he arrived and he told them not to disturb her. It gave Hawker an opportunity to have a word alone with them. Gerald and Phyllis Britwell were highly distressed at their daughter's behaviour since her return. Moody, irascible and withdrawn, she spent most of her time in her room and resisted all offers of company or help. She would not even talk about tennis.

Phyllis was a stately woman in a pale blue dress. Now in her late fifties, she still retained her poise but her handsome features had been ravaged by time and disappointment.

'Katie refused to see the doctor,' she said.

'Is she eating properly?' asked Hawker.

'She won't touch a thing except fruit.'

'That won't do her any harm, Mrs Britwell.'

The couple rehearsed their anxieties then Phyllis withdrew to make tea and to let the men talk on their own. Gerald wore a baggy old cardigan and was nestled into his favourite armchair. The living room at the cottage was low-ceilinged and of medium size. The Britwells had made it cosy and colourful without destroying its character.

'I do appreciate your coming down here, Don.'

'Katie did invite me.'

'You're the only person she wants near her.'

'It must be my aftershave,' joked Hawker.

'I do hope she won't be upset by your appearance,' said Gerald, peering at him. 'When did the accident happen?'

'Not long after you left the hotel.'

'Dear me! It must have been a painful fall.'

'I live to fight another day.'

He had not told the Britwells about the attack on

him. The polite fiction of an accident saved a lot of explanation and he wanted to keep the focus on Katie, not on himself.

'Have the media been bothering you?' he asked.

'They did at first, Don. I kept them at bay.'

'Anyone else been on?'

'Several people. Katie's manager, for one.'

'She's with ISR, isn't she?'

'That's right,' confirmed the old man. 'International Sports Representation. They're part of an American conglomerate. Based in Washington. Jerry Tobias – that's Katie's manager – wanted to fly straight over but I put him off. Jerry is the last person she wants around her at the moment. He'll have to wait until the funeral.'

'When is that?'

'Next Tuesday. The police are releasing the body tomorrow and it's being flown home. There'll be a quiet funeral – immediate family only – then a memorial service in six weeks. You've no idea how difficult it's been to make these arrangements. The police have not been entirely co-operative.'

'I can believe that,' said Hawker with feeling.

'I'll be so relieved when it's all over, Don.'

'Will Katie be up to facing the ordeal?'

'Frankly, no. But we'd never stop her going.'

'Suppose not.'

Hawker's attention wandered to the framed photograph of Katie on the mantlepiece. She was returning a ball from the baseline with a two-handed backhand volley and revelling in the game that she loved.

'What about her decision to give up tennis?' asked Hawker.

'She's sticking by it,' said Gerald, making a wheezing noise. 'I didn't dare mention that to Jerry Tobias or he'd be here right now. It won't be as easy as Katie imagines. She has contractual obligations. If she pulls out completely, she breaks agreements and loses bonuses. The complications are quite mind-boggling, Don.'

'Nobody can force her to play again.'

'That's true.'

'It has to come from inside.'

Footsteps creaked on the oak staircase then Katie herself came into the room. Her obvious pleasure at seeing Hawker was immediately clouded when she noted his injuries.

'My God! What have they done to you?'

'It's not as bad as it looks,' he assured her.

'What happened?'

'I had a slight accident, Katie . . .'

He mollified her with his tale and she calmed down. Phyllis brought in a tray of tea and all four of them chatted together for a while. Then the parents made a tactical withdrawal and left them alone together.

Hawker could see that Katie had been crying again. Glowing from her bath and wearing a neat dress of cream lace, she was patently still weighed down by the burden of her loss. What made it more poignant was the fact that she was clearly making such an effort to appear bright and alert. Since it was all for his benefit, he went along with it.

'You look terrific, Katie.'

'Thanks.'

'How's it been?'

'Not too bad.'

'Glad to be home?'

'Oh, yes,' she said, almost girlishly. 'I'd forgotten how beautiful the garden is in spring. It's something I missed, living in an apartment and moving from hotel to hotel. I promised myself that one day we'd have a house with a big garden. Then Daddy could come to stay with us and potter about to his heart's content.'

'He'd love that.'

'Mel was a city boy,' she explained. 'He didn't

127

understand the appeal of the country. But I would have brought him round.'

'I'm sure.'

'Do you know what he said when he first came here?'

'What?'

Hawker gave her the cue and she talked at length about Mel, recycling memory and anecdote, supplying an occasional strained laugh, somehow trying to persuade herself that it had been a blissfully happy marriage. The longer she went on, the more toll it took on her. The brightness faded from her voice.

There was a long pause. Katie looked pleadingly at him.

'Don?'

'Yes?'

'Did you feel like this when your wife died?'

'Exactly like that.'

'Empty and useless and miserable?'

'It passes in time.'

'Does it?'

'So they tell me.'

Hawker was still waiting to experience the miracle himself.

'How long ago was it?'

'Eight years.'

'Have you thought of marrying again?'

'No, Katie.'

'Never?'

'Out of the question.'

'Why?'

'Because it would be so unfair,' he said. 'I couldn't ask another woman to share all that guilt.'

Katie nodded soulfully.

'Oh, yes. I know about guilt.'

They had been drawn closer together now. Hawker took advantage of the mood to trespass on some delicate territory.

'Drew Grant came to see me.'

'Drew?' She spoke the name as if she had never heard it before.

'He asked after you, Katie.'

'I see.'

'If there's anything he can do . . .' He leaned in closer to her. 'Drew told me about Robert Alexander.'

Katie looked at him in alarm as if he had just struck her.

'He said that Alexander hounded you. According to him —'

'NO!'

Katie's scream silenced him at once and brought her parents scurrying anxiously in. She glanced at them, then back at Hawker, before bursting into tears and running off to the stairs. The bedroom door was soon heard slamming behind her.

Gerald and Phyllis Britwell turned accusingly to their guest.

'I think it's time for me to go,' said Hawker.

It was very late when he got back to Fulham and he had trouble finding a parking place in the street. Eventually, he had to leave his battered old Vauxhall Cavalier two blocks from the flat. The drive back from Hampshire had been spent castigating himself for his lack of tact and commonsense. He had not only managed to upset Katie, he had forfeited her trust and it was vital to have that. Hawker was still punishing himself when he put his key in the front door of the house.

Something lay on the mat in the hallway. He bent down to pick up the brown envelope and saw to his delight that it was from Christina. He rushed up to his room and took the envelope across to his desk, switching on the anglepoise lamp as he dropped into his swivel chair. It had never occurred to him that the photographs would arrive so soon. He was puzzled by the British postmark.

The envelope had arrived at the magazine office. Knowing how anxious Hawker was to receive them, Eric Fretton had sent one of his minions across to Fulham at the end of the working day. Hawker read the editor's writing in the top corner – BY HAND (THANKS, ZOE. I NEEDED THAT). Tearing the envelope open, Hawker took out a pile of glossy proofs that were held together by an elastic band. A cheerful note from Christina explained that she was bribing a Lufthansa stewardess to take the envelope on a flight to Heathrow and post it there. She had put four kisses at the bottom. He would claim them in Rome.

Hawker removed the elastic band and sifted through the thirty or so photographs. Christina Erikkson had been mobile at the Monte Carlo Open. She had got shots of the game from many different angles. Mel Edmunds and Yuri Chegenyov were seen in a variety of positions, not all of them flattering, but Hawker paid no heed to the players. It was the crowd that fascinated him.

Taking a magnifying glass from a drawer, he used it to work his way along the ranks of spectators on all three sides. He soon found them. Guido Barelli was cheering as the Russian took the first set. Lia was applauding, too, but her face was disagreeing with her hands. Vincente sat there with smug satisfaction, his brawny arms folded.

Nance Paulson was up on the terrace during a later stage of the game. She was absorbed in the contest, watching with a professional's eye. Her husband, however, exhibited nothing but disgust. Jean-Louis Croizier was staring down at the court as if there was something particularly unpleasant down there. The faces of Alain Dupont and Dimitri confirmed that Mel Edmunds must have been on top at that point. The artist propped himself up on the table in an attitude of languid disdain. He seemed to be challenging Mel to impress him then scorning the efforts. Dimitri was the most involved of them all.

But his mind was not on the tennis.

Hawker searched on and saw other people he recognized. He was interested to see Henri Lequesne in the crowd and rather nonplussed when he found the visage of Raoul Chabrier. There were other players from the tournament with girlfriends, coaches and general hangers-on. He was amused to see several shots of himself, gazing around anxiously early on, more relaxed when Katie Britwell was beside him.

A new photograph gave him a different perspective of the match. It also gave him a shock that made him sit up. In the heart of the crowd behind the umpire's chair was a face that had no reason to be there.

It was Drew Grant.

Chapter Five

Anger fuelled his game throughout the tournament. Yuri Chegenyov not only coasted through to the final, he won it in straight sets at a blistering pace. Dilip Nayar, the brilliant Indian player, was reduced to shuffling anonymity on court. He simply could not cope with the Russian's speed and strength and savagery. Chegenyov was on fire.

Watching from the stand, Alex Kutsk was delighted. It was more than just another tournament victory. His player had shown himself to be a worthy successor to Mel Edmunds. For the first time ever, the flag of the Soviet Union would flutter atop the world tennis rankings. He thought of the kudos it would gain Chegenyov back home. Banquets, honours and gifts would be heaped upon him. As the person who had masterminded the player's career, Alex himself would get his share of the spoils. The future was sweet with promise.

'Magnificent, Yuri!' he congratulated.

'Thanks.'

'You have never played better.'

Chegenyov had never been that angry before. He let Alex burble on at him as he got out of his sodden tennis wear. When the player stepped under the shower, the coach scuttled off to gather his things for departure. Chegenyov had been trying to engineer another meeting with Christina Erikkson all week but he had been foiled. He wanted to make one last bid. Showering quickly, he changed into his clothes and rushed straight back out on the court, hoping that she might be lingering around with some of the others. But Christina was not there.

His anger crackled inside him once again.

Alex had laid on transport to Hamburg airport and they arrived in good time for the flight to Moscow. The coach was buoyant but the player was surly and subdued. Chegenyov waved away autograph hunters with uncharacteristic rudeness. The importance of pleasing his public had been drilled into him but he chose to forget it for once.

'What is wrong, Yuri?' demanded Alex. 'You win a victory.'

'But I cannot stay to celebrate it.'

'We celebrate it in Moscow.'

'It is not the same.'

'This is a great day for us, Yuri. Be happy.'

But the player remained annoyed and resentful.

Security at the airport was intense. After going through passport control, they had to endure a body search before being allowed into the departure lounge. Males and females split up to go into their respective booths for the search. Chegenyov stood in the queue behind his coach and took a desultory interest in what was going on. Alex then went into the booth.

'Hi there!' called a voice.

'Oh. Hello.'

'Fantastic match. You were out of this world.'

Christina Erikkson had just joined the queue for the other booth. Though they were separated by fifteen yards and talking in public, Chegenyov was nevertheless thrilled. Chance had contrived what he had not. She saw him, she liked him, she spoke to him. Somehow it redeemed the whole week for him.

'Where are you going?' she asked.

'Moscow.'

'I'm off to Rome.'

'Me, too, in a week's time.'

'See you there, maybe.'

It was a casual remark when Christina made it but it became a firm promise by the time it reached the Russian. His face split in a grin. The curtain was pulled back on the booth and a uniformed customs officer beckoned him in. Chegenyov looked over his shoulder.

'I look forward to it, Christina.'

'Good.'

'Enjoy your flight!'

'And you!'

He stepped into the booth and the curtain screened him from view. Christina dismissed him from her mind and started chatting to the woman behind her. She had no idea how significant the dialogue had been to Chegenyov.

Unwittingly, she had helped to change his life.

Alain Dupont had always been methodical about his work. He stuck to certain hours of the day when the light was at its best, and he did not permit any interruption to his routine when he was involved with a new painting. His output was still prolific and it attracted the familiar accusations of being facile and shallow, but his commissions continued to flow in and his paintings graced the walls of galleries and private collections all over the globe.

Punctilious about detail, he spent a long time setting it all up in his studio. The sofa had to be at the right angle, the carpet of the right colour and texture, the other items arranged for dramatic effect. Sunlight was now flooding into the studio which was at the rear of his villa in Monte Carlo. It was time to begin but there was only one thing missing. It would complete the picture in every way.

Alain crossed to the door and called up the stairs.

'Dimitri!'

'I'm coming!'

'Don't keep me waiting.'

'Here I am.'

'Ah!' It was a sigh of pleasure.

'Well?'

The young Greek was posing at the top of the stairs in a white bathrobe. His swarthy face, hands and legs were thrown into relief. Light from the window directly behind him gave him a halo effect. Alain drank it all in and clapped his hands softly in admiration.

'Bravo!'

'You like?'

'I like, Dimitri!'

Descending the stairs with slow movements, Dimitri went past him into the studio. He moved to the sofa, draped himself across it and let the bathrobe part slightly. Alain hurried across to his easel to enjoy a closer and more privileged view.

'How do you want me?' asked the young man.

Janice was using the word processor when she heard the knock on the door.

'Come in!' she invited, preparing her smile.

'Good afternoon.'

'Oh, my God!'

The sight of Hawker's face could still disturb. If anything, the black eye looked even more sensational now that it was acquiring a yellow tinge. Janice collected herself and stood up.

'I do beg your pardon, sir?'

'I walked into a lamp-post,' he explained.

'Is Mr Alexander expecting you?'

'Don Hawker. Four o'clock.'

'Come this way, please.'

'Thanks.'

135

He was shown into a modern, well-appointed office and left alone. Hawker noted the exceptional tidiness of the desk and compared it with the chaos of his own working environment at the flat. Tennis posters lined one wall and Katie Britwell was featured on the largest of them. There was also a calendar, a flow chart and a map of the world. The sign on the back of the door was large and unequivocal – NO SMOKING. It was the office of a man who liked to control his air space.

Hawker knew that the International Tennis Federation had used accommodation at Wimbledon for some years but it had now moved back to West London. There was far less sense of history than at the All-England Club and no adjacent courts to conjure up memories, but other considerations weighed. For all its dizzy eminence, Wimbledon was mainly concerned with the staging of an event that occupied only a fortnight in the tennis year. The ITF, by contrast, was continuously involved in the administration of the international game and thus operated on a global scale. Having its own suite of offices gave it a necessary independence.

A copy of the *ITF News* lay folded neatly on the desk. It was the organization's quarterly newspaper and Hawker picked it up with interest. The front page was devoted to the Federation Cup, the major international team championship for women players. Over forty nations were competing in the forthcoming event which was to be hosted by Czechoslovakia. There was a plan of the tennis complex on Stvanice Island in the middle of the River Vltava in Prague. Beneath it was a photograph of the current holders of the Federation Cup – the United States team. Nance Paulson, Jody Beecher, Pat Estevez and Ingrid Bellinghausen wore victory smiles. It was a formidable quartet.

Hawker was about to read on when the door opened. He put the paper down again as Robert

Alexander breezed in. Smartly dressed in a double-breasted suit of grey flannel, he peered over the top of half-moon spectacles at his visitor.

'Don Hawker?'

'How do you do, Mr Alexander?'

'Pleased to meet you. Take a pew.'

In one brisk movement, Robert shook his hand, indicated the upright chair, closed the door, stepped behind his desk and removed his glasses. Several inches shorter than Hawker, he remained on his feet while the other sat. With a polite smile, he appraised his guest shrewdly. Hawker observed that he was far too well-bred to make an issue of his facial disfigurement.

Robert's manner was pleasant but businesslike.

'As I explained over the telephone, I can't give you much time today, I'm afraid. We're into a rather hectic period.'

'I understand.'

'Another meeting at four-thirty, in fact.'

'Good of you to see me at such short notice.'

'I'll help all I can, dear chap.'

He sat down in his high-backed chair and toyed with his glasses. Hawker decided that they were an affectation and that his companion could see perfectly well without them. It was another strike against the man. One of many.

'How are you finding the wonderful world of tennis?' said Robert.

'Fascinating.'

'Finest game ever invented.'

'It certainly has its attractions.'

'The acme of sporting endeavour.'

'If only it wasn't so confusing.'

'Confusing?'

'I don't mean the game itself,' said Hawker. 'It's all those organizations tied in with it. ITF. ATP. MIPTC.

BLTA. WITA. And so on. I was lost in a forest of initials at first.'

'It can be somewhat bewildering,' agreed Robert, 'but one soon learns. International Tennis Federation. Association of Tennis Professionals. Men's International Professional Tennis Council. British Lawn Tennis Association. Women's International Tennis Association. Bit of a mouthful, aren't they? You can see why we fall back on initials.'

'Do you get much conflict of interest?'

'Between them? All the time.'

'Who has the final say?'

'We like to think that we do.'

There was a smugness that offended Hawker, the well-mannered arrogance of someone who enjoyed the position of power he held in the sport. Hawker sought to puncture his quiet self-importance.

'Do you play tennis yourself?'

'Whenever I have the opportunity.'

'Were you a pro?'

'Alas, no.'

'Then how can you begin to understand their problems?'

'There is such a thing as empathy,' said the other urbanely. 'I flatter myself that I have real insight into the vicissitudes of life on the professional circuit. It's not as if I'm a complete novice. I did win Junior Wimbledon in my youth. It's just that I feel I can serve the game more effectively as an administrator. The action is not confined to the tennis court, I can assure you. We have our share.'

Hawker felt as if he had been put in his place and it made him squirm. Robert Alexander's condescending civility was too much to bear. It was time for a more direct assault on him.

'I've been working with Katie Britwell and Mel Edmunds.'

'I do read the papers, Mr Hawker.'

'Then you'll know I've been in Monte Carlo.'

'With sensational effect.'

'There's more to it than that, Mr Alexander.'

'So I hear.'

'What?'

'Quentin Rivers and I are members of the same club.'

It explained a lot. Hawker knew he had met the patronising tone before. He began to feel uneasy because he was wearing a light jerkin and slacks. His dress sense was under silent bombardment. He wished he had worn a tie. The other's immaculate appearance put him at a disadvantage.

'Yes,' continued Robert blithely. 'Quentin tells me that you didn't exactly endear yourself with the bona fide tennis correspondents. They found you a trifle bullish. Quentin called you the "Tough of the Track". The reference was lost on me, I fear.'

'Alf Tupper,' said Hawker. 'Character in a kid's comic.'

'Before my time.'

'Used to eat fish and chips then go off to win mile races.'

'I see what Quentin was getting at.'

Class was pushing them apart with every sentence.

'Let's get down to the nitty-gritty, shall we?' suggested Hawker.

'Is that what Alf Tupper used to say?'

'I believe you know Katie.'

'Everyone in tennis knows her.'

'You're a friend of hers?'

'I like to think so.'

'An unwanted friend.'

'I object to that phrase, Mr Hawker.'

'He said you would.'

'Who did?'

'Drew Grant.'

A flicker of irritation showed in Robert's face. He put his glasses on so that he could look over the top of them again.

'What exactly are you after, Mr Hawker?'

'The truth.'

'In abstract terms?'

'Why did Katie break off her engagement?'

'There's an easy answer to that one.'

'Is there?'

'Drew Grant was pathologically unsuitable.'

'Then why did they become engaged in the first place?'

'I wish I knew,' said Robert seriously.

'Drew was rather scathing about you, Mr Alexander.'

'Indeed?'

'According to him – '

'Look here,' interrupted Robert. 'Let me tell you straight away that Grant has a vastly higher opinion of *me* than I do of *him*. He was a competent player in his day but that's all he was. As a potential husband, he was totally unworthy of Katie. The man has no style, no breeding, no integrity.'

'That's a bit harsh.'

'Our time is running out, Mr Hawker.'

'Why did you pursue Katie?'

'I have no idea what you're talking about.'

'You hounded her.'

'Is this conversation really necessary?'

'Drew called it an obsession.'

'Really?'

'You first met Katie at a Federation Cup match, didn't you?'

'That happens to be my area of responsibility,' said Robert with easy pomposity. 'The Federation Cup takes me all over the world. I have regular contact with the British team. For some years now, Katie has been its leading light.'

140

Hawker could not get through his guard. He was far too well-defended and his voice betrayed no emotion. It was not hard to see why Drew Grant and Robert Alexander were enemies. Even without a rivalry over Katie Britwell, they would never have been soul mates.

'May I ask *you* a question?' said Robert.

'Sure.'

'Have you spoken to Katie since she came back?'

'Yes.'

'How is she?' Formal politeness hid genuine concern.

'A bit shell-shocked.'

'Naturally. Did she say anything at all about me?'

'No.'

'Made no complaints or allegations?'

'None.'

'So all you're going on is the word of Drew Grant.'

'Supported by my own observation.'

Another flicker of irritation. Robert got to his feet to signal that the interview was over. Remaining in his seat, Hawker fired a shot across his bows.

'I think she got engaged to Drew as a means of escape.'

'From whom?'

'You.'

'Janice will show you out.'

'Just answer this – why did she marry Mel Edmunds?'

The mask cracked slightly for the first time and Hawker caught a glimpse of pain and humiliation. Robert Alexander quickly recovered himself. His manner was at its most patronizing.

'Oh, I think Mel had a certain tawdry glamour, don't you?' he said. 'A tabloid charm. A crude attraction. Mel Edmunds was the romantic equivalent of junk food. Always available, but injurious to health in the long run. And we must never forget his record. He was, after all, a legend. In more ways than one. Katie must have been dazzled by him. I can't think why else she could bear to be in the same room with Mel.'

Hawker rose from his chair and met the condescending gaze.

'You and Rivers must have some rare old times at the club?'

'Goodbye, Mr Hawker.'

'Tearing other human beings into little strips from the comfort of your leather armchairs. Tell me, is there anyone that you actually *like*?' Hawker opened the door wide. 'And for the record, Quentin Rivers is not a bona fide tennis correspondent. He's a public school piss-artist who plays a wonderful game of tennis with a glass of gin in his hand.'

Robert subjected him to a supercilious stare.

'I believe you have to go and buy fish and chips.'

'Back to the Tough of the Track, are we?'

'If the cap fits.'

'There's something you ought to know about Alf Tupper.'

'I doubt it.'

'He always came out on top in the end.'

Robert dispatched him with a cold smile and closed the door after him. His control vanished as he plopped back down into his chair and he banged the desk hard with both fists. Breathing heavily through his nose, he glanced up at the poster of Katie Britwell. It strengthened his resolve. He had gone too far to back down now. Don Hawker was a problem that had to be solved and he would find the way.

Robert Alexander would not be thwarted at the last hurdle.

After following the sun around America for a few months, the Virginia Slims Women's Tour came to Europe at the start of May. Rome provided a radiant welcome. The players converged on the Foro Italico, one of the game's most exciting and volatile arenas, for a tournament that was stimulating immense public interest. Most of the big names were there. Nance Paulson was back after injury. Jody Beecher was on a high after her recent victory in Houston. Anna Portizkova, the dour Czech, had hit form. Laura Lennig carried German hopes. Ingrid Bellinghausen always played well in Rome. And one of the new stars on the circuit, Sara Clarino, fearless, talented and hungry for success, aroused local passions by promising that she would do everything within her power to win the Italian Open for the home country.

Only Katie Britwell was missing, an absence that cast a slight shadow over the event. There was enormous sympathy for her among the players and disappointment among the fans. If anyone could stop the rolling juggernaut known as Nance Paulson, it was the British player but hushed rumours were already circulating that she might not rejoin the tour at all. The death of her husband had robbed her of all motivation and commitment to the game.

The early stages of the tournament adhered strictly to the form book. Paulson surged on. Beecher flourished. Portizkova stuck to her task remorselessly. Lennig shone. Bellinghausen enhanced her cause. Sara Clarino kept Italian heads high with a scintillating performance against Patti Baff, only to suffer the narrowest of defeats in her quarter-final against Lori Vincent, another seasoned Australian. The delirious home crowd acclaimed their heroine as if she had won the title and she waved her thanks to them. During the next match, the same spectators around the centre court showed that they could hiss as well as cheer. Laura Lennig took on Rafaella Perez of Mexico and the slow Italian clay reduced their encounter to a series of dull, repetitive, never-ending rallies. Whistles and boos accompanied the extended boredom as the fans became increasingly restive. They wanted action.

Don Hawker arrived in Rome in time to catch the semi-final between Nance Paulson and Jody Beecher. Sitting in the Press Box, he took care to stay well clear of Quentin Rivers. Hawker's face was now returning to something like its normal shape, but the long gash on his forehead – freed from its covering plaster and deprived of its stitches – gave him a piratical air. He hoped that he would soon be able to discuss his injuries with the person who gave them to him.

The match was a sizzler and the crowd was in a frenzy before the end of the first set. Jody Beecher was a revelation. Off court, she had the shy, winsome, don't-hit-me look of a victim but she turned predator once the first game was under way. She swooped viciously on every ball and sent it zinging back over the net. What fired the spectators was her do-or-die attitude. She simply never gave up.

It was vastly entertaining and went to three sets. In the end, the Paulson power was decisive. Hawker had seen more stylish players but few as mercilessly effective. Nance always had tactical control and much more in reserve when it counted. After an hour and a half in the baking sun, she was still serving with unabated ferocity and she took the final point with a glorious ace. The reigning queen of the women's game could still put ambitious princesses in their place.

Jody Beecher took her defeat gracefully. Nance ran to the net to shake her hand, kiss her on the cheek and lead her across to the umpire. The fans gave them a rapturous ovation and the photographers moved in swiftly. It was an altogether more boisterous scene than any at the Monte Carlo Open and Hawker was caught up in the bubbling hysteria. The Foro Italico was pure amphitheatre.

Wedged in amongst her colleagues from various nations, Christina Erikkson made sure that she had her share of close-ups. When the two players finally left the court and the din subsided, she looked up to the Press Box. Hawker waved to her. Using an elaborate semaphore, they agreed to meet outside later on.

Hawker left the box and headed for an exit.

'Did you enjoy the match, M'sieur?'

'Very much.'

'Mademoiselle Beecher will be a champion one day.'

'Not for a long while yet,' said Hawker. 'Nance will see to that.

'Madame Croizier was *magnifique*!'

Chief Inspector Yves Daninos had contrived to intercept him in a gangway. The policeman wore a natty lightweight suit and an open-necked shirt. Hawker was surprised to see him.

'I didn't know you liked tennis,' he said.

'I don't. But I like tennis players – that kind, anyway.'

'The ladies do have a special appeal, don't they?'

'I have been watching some of the others practice on the outside courts,' confided Daninos. 'So much beauty on the move. I can see why Monsieur Edmunds was so tempted.' He became solicitous. 'How is she?'

'Katie? I haven't seen her for a while,' admitted Hawker.

'You have spoken with her?'

'With her father,' said the other. 'The funeral was a trial for both of them but they got through it. Katie is back at home.'

'It is probably the best place for her.'

They were clogging up the gangway and people were pushing past them to get out. Daninos pointed to the exit and motioned Hawker to follow. They made their way to a quiet corner behind the stadium. Pine trees rustled in the whispering wind. Birds sang in the heat.

The policeman studied his face to check his wounds.

'You look almost human again, M'sieur.'

'Thanks.'

'Still no idea who did this to you?'

'None at all,' he lied.

'I thought not.' He became conspiratorial. 'I have been talking with Monsieur Edmunds' manager. Do you know how much that young man made last year?'

'Little bit more than me, I daresay,' ventured Hawker.

'Well over a million dollars.'

'That's the going rate for the top man these days.'

'Doesn't it hurt you, M'sieur?'

'Hurt?'

'To see someone getting so much for so little.'

'Oh, come on,' argued Hawker. 'Mel was a magical player.'

'Maybe. But you cannot compare him with a Pavarotti.'

'How good is *he* with a tennis racket?'

'We should reward the right people in this world,' argued the detective seriously. 'Art is more important than sport.'

'Watch Mel Edmunds and you got both at the same time.' Hawker was into his stride. 'It doesn't worry me how much he earned. What I find disgusting is the long queue of people waiting to take their slice of it. All big money sports are the same. Too many managers, agents, legal advisers, consultants, promoters, fixers, middlemen and other parasites in search of a fat percentage.'

'Someone has to organize a sport.'

'Organization is one thing: exploitation is quite another.'

'You are an idealist, M'sieur.'

'A sport should exist for those who play it.'

'And a romantic.'

146

'Take tennis as an example,' said Hawker, warming to his theme. 'Mel was handled by ISR, one of the biggest agencies in the world. When they promote a tournament themselves, they make sure there are plenty of their own players involved. That way, they can maximize their take.'

'Take?'

Hawker used his fingers to count off the various items.

'ISR get a fee as manager of the event,' he began. 'They get a percentage of the sponsorship fee. A percentage of the prize money won by their players. A percentage of any on-site endorsement money earned by those players. A percentage of the income realized from any merchandise sold. A fee for selling the television broadcast. A fee for producing the telecast. A fee for selling the advertising on the telecast. A fee for providing television commentary. And that's only the start of it!'

'I did not ask for a lecture, M'sieur,' said Daninos.

'I'm sorry. It's a subject that gets to me.'

'So I notice.'

'The point I'm making is that a lot of people made a lot of money out of Mel Edmunds. Some of them are not very nice people. Most of them are not necessary.'

'But Monsieur Edmunds was still a wealthy man.'

'A millionaire. Six or seven times over.'

'That is the point *I* am making.'

'What?'

'Somebody must inherit all that money.'

Hawker blinked. He had missed the obvious. His concern had been to help Katie through her darkest days and to ease the sense of loss. But there were gains as well and he saw them for the first time.

Chief Inspector Yves Daninos rammed home his point.

'She can retire as a very rich woman. She does not need to play this strange game ever again.'

Gerald Britwell was doing some gentle weeding in the garden before the light started to fade. He worked with his hoe then put the weeds into his plastic wheelbarrow. Gnats buzzed. The dog cavorted around the lawn. Somewhere in the distance, an electric hedge-trimmer could be heard.

He did not see Katie come out of the cottage.

'I've brought you a cup of tea, Daddy,' she said.

'Marvellous! Thanks, darling.'

'Don't overdo it, Mummy says.'

'As always.' He took the cup and sipped. 'Ah. You made this.'

'How can you tell?'

'Real sugar. Your mother will insist on putting those dreadful artificial sweeteners in. I detest them.'

Katie smiled. It was several days since the funeral now and she was starting to come out of her trance. Time had passed by aimlessly for her. It was almost the first time she had wandered into the garden.

'Lovely to see you out here,' he said.

'It looked so peaceful.'

'Fancy a spot of weeding?'

'No thanks.'

'Watch me then. I'll show you how it's done.'

'I'll just walk around for a bit,' she decided.

'Why not take a stroll up through the village?'

'I'm not ready for that yet.'

She walked slowly down the path, studying the flowerbeds on either side, pausing occasionally to touch or sniff. Gerald watched her with misgivings. His daughter's withdrawal had continued. She just wanted to cut herself off from everything and everybody. Many people had rung or written or called on the off-chance of seeing her but Katie had ignored them all. Simply to get her out of the cottage was an achievement.

Katie stepped on to the lawn and immediately secured the interest of the dog. Penny was a young golden-haired Labrador. She had been trained not to vandalize the garden or to rush out on the road but she was still full of animal high spirits. Bounding up to Katie, she put paws up on her thighs. Katie patted her head then eased her to the ground. Penny went after her as she crossed the lawn, wagging her tail furiously as if joining in some game.

Gerald was worried that the dog might be a nuisance but Katie seemed to tolerate her. Indeed, when she reached the grove of sycamores, Katie bent down to pick up a small stick. Penny lunged for it at once. Katie pulled it away then threw it a short distance. The dog raced over to it and scooped it up in its jaws before taking it back. It was the start of a harmless game between them.

Katie threw the stick further each time and Penny retrieved it with panting willingness. The stick was eventually hurled into the paddock and landed in some bushes. The dog was defeated for a moment and circled wildly, barking noisily. Katie went to see what had happened but she soon forgot all about the dog.

The tennis court confronted her. It looked rather neglected now and its net lay slack between the uprights. Tufts of grass were poking up between the tarmac and there was rust on the wire netting. But the court was redolent with memories for her. As a girl, she had played hundreds and hundreds of games on it with her friends. Even as a fully-fledged professional, she always spent some time on the court whenever she came home and she had grown accustomed to its little undulations. It was rather sad to see that the line-markings were fading in places.

Katie stared at it for some time until she realized

with a start when it had last been used. Mel and she had visited the cottage just before they had got married and they spent a happy hour on a Sunday morning just playing for the fun of it.

Gerald Britwell came up to her shoulder.

'We can get it tidied up in no time, darling.'

'No, thanks.'

'Are you sure?'

She nodded, kissed him on the cheek then went back indoors.

Jean-Louis Croizier was in Rome to see his wife and his sportswear win the Italian Open. Anna Poritzkova had provided a stern test for one set then buckled slightly under the continuous onslaught. Whatever problems Nance had with her elbow were now behind her. She exhibited all her old power and fluency. As the moment of victory came, she raised her racket in the air and turned to look up at her husband. He beamed happily and blew her a kiss.

Bellecroix had another victory to its name.

Hawker kept an eye on Jean-Louis as he made his way down to the court side. Relaxed, assured and unassuming, he chatted with the officials and waited until Nance escaped from the ring of photographers. A few of them had their cameras ready when he gave his wife a congratulatory kiss. They were a winning team in every sense. Nance was glowing with exhilaration. Jean-Louis was taking a quiet pleasure in it all.

The owner of Bellecroix Sportswear exuded charm but Hawker was not taken in by it for a moment. He knew that the real monsters were always exceptionally nice people on the surface. Jean-Louis Croizier fascinated him. He found himself wondering how much the Frenchman would pay to have someone murdered.

What price would a Mel Edmunds have fetched?

Hawker did not stay for the doubles final. The

pairing of Nance Paulson and Jody Beecher made it a foregone conclusion. He decided to do some sightseeing instead and give himself time to think. He felt that he was getting closer to solving the mystery. Vague ideas were firming up into proven fact. Educated guesses were hitting their target. Intuition was guiding him in the right direction.

His limited budget obliged him once again to stay in very modest accommodation. Christina Erikkson, on the other hand, was at the luxury hotel where most of the players had been billeted. She persuaded him to join her for dinner there that evening and teased him with going back on his principles. But Hawker had a good reason to come to the hotel. It enabled him to mix with the players and their entourage.

'Besides,' he insisted, 'I pay the bill.'

'Let me charge it to expenses.'

'This is personal. I pick up the tab.'

'You think I'm worth it, Hawker?'

'We'll find out later.'

They lapsed back into the easy, unforced relationship of Monte Carlo. It was very restorative. Christina even began to get used to the unsightly alterations to his face.

'I love that scar on your forehead.'

'That's why I had it put there.'

'And that mark on your cheek.'

'A love-bite from Monte Carlo.'

'You look exotic.'

'I've never been called that before.'

'Take me to my room,' she hissed.

'I'm still eating.'

'Eat *me* instead.'

It was a treat to be with Christina. She wore an attractive white dress with blue edging and buttons. Her hair was pinned up at the back the way he liked it and he fantasized about removing the slides later on so that it cascaded down around her naked shoulders. They sat at a table in the corner and enjoyed an excellent view of the restaurant as well as fine Italian cuisine.

Lots of the players were in evidence. Nance Paulson presided over a table of seven and had them rocking with laughter at her stories. Jean-Louis was quite happy to sit back and let her enjoy the limelight. His was essentially a supporting role that evening. Ingrid Bellinghausen shared a table with Jody Beecher and Cathy Wyman, another American on the circuit. The young man with them seemed to be chatting them all up assiduously but Hawker could not work out with whom he had come.

Patti Baff and Lori Vincent were dining with two of the Italian officials. The animated quartet formed a picture that provided its own caption. Latin gallantry was merging with Australian directness. Laura Lennig was alone with her German husband and Anna Poritzkova with her coach. As the women moved on from Rome, the men took their place and there were a few early arrivals. The most notable of these was Yuri Chegenyov who came into the restaurant with a heady optimism that perished the moment he saw Christina Erikkson with a man. He rallied slightly when she waved then got whisked off to a table by Alex Kutsk. The Russian player sat morose and doe-eyed.

Hawker was amused at all the by-play.

'What's wrong with Yuri?'

'I think he fancies me.'

'Can't blame him there.'

'He wants to get laid and doesn't know how to go about it.'

'That coach of his acts as a chaperone.'

'Mm. Pity.'

'Why?'

'I've never done it with a Russian before.'

152

'But he's a Communist,' protested Hawker.

'Not with his clothes off.'

They laughed and went back to their food. Yuri Chegenyov continued to stare dolefully across at her and Christina rewarded him with a smile or a nod from time to time.

Hawker got his bonus while choosing a dessert. There was a flurry of interest and he looked up to see Guido Barelli sailing into the restaurant with the gorgeous Sara Clarino on his arm. Any hint of scandal was removed by the fact that they were accompanied by three high-ranking Italian officials who were there to wine and dine the two leading players in the country. Some photographs were taken at their table then they settled down to their meal.

Barelli was not alone. Coming back to Italy always posed some problems for him. He was feted like a pop star and pursued by gaggles of teenage girls. Keeping them at bay was the pleasant task of his bodyguard and Hawker could see Vincente just inside the bar that was adjacent to the restaurant. He was within reach of his master.

Hawker did not rush. He lingered over his dessert and coffee then ordered a liqueur for Christina. They had plenty to talk about and an hour slipped by without their noticing it. People began to drift away from their tables. Patti Baff and Lori Vincent went off with their escorts to cement international relations. Nance Paulson adjourned to the lounge with her friends so that she could hold court there. And Yuri Chegenyov was hustled through his meal before being taken away by Alex Kutsk who had now identified Christina as a high risk factor. Others floated off until only a few tables were occupied. Most of the diners were now women. It was a crucial help to Hawker's plan.

Guido Barelli was in his element. Flattered by the

officials and flirting with Sara Clarino, he laughed his
way through a meal that was washed down by regular
glasses of red wine. It was only a question of time before
he had to excuse himself from the table. Hawker let him
go out then rose to follow.

'Are we leaving?' asked Christina.

'Not yet. I have to see someone.'

'Who?'

'Barelli.'

'Why?'

'To annoy him.'

The gentleman's toilet was at the end of a corridor off
the restaurant. Nobody else was about. No heavy traffic
was due in the near future. He waited until the door
opened then walked towards it, stopping in surprise as
he confronted Barelli.

'*Permesso, signor*,' said the Italian.

'Guido Barelli?'

'*Si*.'

'I'm Don Hawker. A journalist from England.'

'Ah. How do you do?'

Barelli produced the reflex smile he kept for
anyone from the press and exchanged a handshake. His
English was poor but intelligible.

'You like Roma, signor!'

'Very much.'

'Stay next week,' advised Barelli. 'Maybe I win, eh?'

'Don't bank on it.'

'What you say?'

'Chegenyov can beat you in his sleep,' urged Hawker.
'In fact, I heard that you pulled out of that tournament
in Hamburg because you were afraid to play him.'

'Guido Barelli is afraid of nobody!'

'That's what they're saying.'

'My mother was ill. I was needed here.'

'That's only part of the truth,' said Hawker.

'Why?'

154

'Because you still managed to fit in two exhibition matches that week. One in Turin, one in Geneva. Perhaps your mother made a recovery for those two days.'

'Who *are* you?' demanded Barelli, fuming.

'A friend of Mel Edmunds. Not the only one, it seems.'

'What you mean?'

'Your wife knew him as well, didn't she?'

'Shut your mouth, signor!'

'She wanted a number one player for a change.'

Barelli snorted with rage and looked as if he was about to hit Hawker, but he stayed his hand and issued forth a stream of expletives in Italian. Realization dawned. He pointed a finger.

'Hawker, did you say?'

'That's me.'

'You ring Lia. Upset her. My wife tell me.'

'I just wanted a chat about Mel, that's all.'

'Be quiet about him!'

'He was another player you were scared of, wasn't he?'

'No!'

'You hated Mel.'

'Yes, I hate him.'

'Because he was better than you,' prodded Hawker. 'And not only on the tennis court!'

Barelli looked as if he were about to explode. His eyes went black, his teeth were clenched and veins stood out on his temples. Sweeping Hawker violently aside, he charged off down the corridor. The first part of the plan had worked to perfection. Hawker now went quickly into the toilet to check that it was empty. Then he filled a basin with water before pulling several paper towels from the dispenser. He was pretending to wash his hands when the door burst open. One eye stayed on the mirror in front of him.

Vincente took in the situation and grinned. Closing the door behind him, he made a sudden rush at Hawker's back but the latter was ready for him. Instead of grappling with his prey, the bodyguard found a pile of soggy paper thrust into his face. A left hook made his ear ring and a second punch split his lip. The Italian howled in fury and hurled the paper away.

Circling his opponent, he looked for an opening. But Hawker knew how to take care of himself in a fight. He also had the advantage of surprise. Vincente was a wrestler. Hawker knew what to expect. But the bodyguard did not. This was proved when Hawker stepped in with a series of punches to the face and body that shook the big man. When he tried to grab his assailant, Vincente found him much too nimble.

'Not so easy this time, is it?' said Hawker.

The Italian circled again, making a rasping sound as he did so.

'I haven't got my back turned at the Hotel Brassard.'

Only a wrestler would hit him with a forearm and that is what Hawker had seen coming at him in that split-second of consciousness on the concrete steps. Vincente's forearm smash could bend a steel lamp-post. In the photograph of the Monte Carlo Open, the bodyguard had been sitting with his massive arms folded. It had been a painful reminder for Hawker.

Vincente charged and grabbed at Hawker's coat. A knee came up into his stomach and knocked the wind out of him. As he released his man, Vincente had to withstand another barrage of blows. His old ring-craft came to his aid and he shammed dizziness. When Hawker moved in to deal out more punishment, a scything foot suddenly knocked him off balance. Vincente followed, caught hold of his arm and swung him across the room. Hawker fell to the floor and rolled over.

He was just in time to see a foot aimed at his face. Moving his head sharply, he grabbed the foot and yanked it with all his might. The bulky frame of the Italian thundered to the floor. Hawker was up in a flash to get in a kick of his own into the groin. Vincente cried in agony and sat up to put both hands to his crotch. Hawker was not finished with him yet. Summoning up all his strength, he took hold of the other's collar and dragged him to his feet. Vincente was unable to resist when his own weight was used against him.

One hand on his neck and the other on the seat of the Italian's trousers, Hawker ran him the full width of the room and smashed his head against the tiled wall. There was a sickening thud and blood spurted everywhere. Vincente went down in a groaning heap. Hawker turned him over with his foot and looked down at the fallen giant. Then he used both hands to scoop up some water from the basin and throw it over the moaning figure. Hawker was about to leave when a strange thing happened.

Vincente laughed. A low, grim chuckle of self-mockery.

Lying in a pool of his own blood, he gave Hawker a lopsided grin. It was a sportsman's acknowledgement of a superior opponent. It was something else as well. A clear warning. They had clashed twice now and each had won a round. They were quits.

The decider was yet to come.

Hawker went out into the corridor and adjusted his clothes. Wrapping a handkerchief around his bleeding knuckles, he thrust the hand into his pocket so that it would be out of sight. Then he went back into the restaurant with as much nonchalance as he could manage, tossing a meaningful glance to Barelli and getting enormous satisfaction out of the response. The Italian was literally goggling with disbelief.

157

Christina looked up with mild impatience.

'What kept you?'

'I bumped into a friend.'

'Where are we going now?'

'Your room.'

'Why?'

'To make love.'

Hawker felt that he had earned it.

Alain Dupont finished work at his usual time and put his brushes aside. The painting was now at quite an advanced stage and he was pleased with it. While Dimitri went off to change, he cleared his things away before washing his hands. He was enjoying a glass of sparkling wine when his young friend returned. Dimitri was handed his own glass.

'To good old Yorkshire!' said Alain.

'Yorkshire!'

They clinked glasses and drank deep. Alain twinkled.

'I must take you there one day.'

'It is nice?'

'Beautiful, Dimitri. Listen to this.'

He crossed to the Bang and Olufsen cabinet and put on a record. Brass band music soon filled the room with comic incongruity. Yorkshire colliers were putting all their puff into a traditional air.

'Ilkley Moor,' said the artist.

'Where?'

'I'll show you one day.'

Alain enjoyed the music for a while then clicked his fingers.

'I almost forgot!'

'What?'

'I have a present.'

'For me?' Dimitri's white teeth came into view.

'You've been such a dear boy to me.'

'What is it? Where is it?'

'Don't be in such a rush,' teased the other.

'Is it a good present?'

'Nothing very special. Just a token.'

He led the way to the front of the house and opened the door. Dimitri gaped. Standing in the forecourt was a brand new Ferrari with gleaming red bodywork. He was overcome with emotion.

'This is . . . mine?'

'Well, I certainly don't want the damn thing.'

'It's wonderful, Alain!'

'You did say you liked red.'

'I cannot believe it is mine.'

'Perhaps these will convince you.'

Alain Dupont took some ignition keys from his pocket and handed them over. Dimitri was beside himself. He walked around the car and stroked the bodywork with light fingers. Then he came back to Alain and embraced him. The artist patted his back softly.

'There, there, dear heart. You deserve it.'

'Do I?'

'Of course,' said the artist. 'You did something very important for me. I always repay that kind of service.'

'Thank you, Alain! Thank you, thank you!'

'I do have an ulterior motive, mind you.'

'What?'

'I want to see the French Open next week.'

'Oh.'

'Dimitri – you can drive me to Paris!'

Robert Alexander worked late at the office then dropped off for an hour at his club. It was well past ten when he headed for home. Swinging on to the forecourt of the flats, he parked his Porsche in its allotted place and got out with his briefcase. Before he could move, a figure stepped out of the shadows to accost him.

'I want a word with you, Alexander!'

It was Drew Grant. The long wait had exacerbated him.

'Do you mind getting out of my way,' returned Robert.

'Keep away from Katie!'

'Is that your advice or hers?'

'Mine.'

'Then you know what you can do with it, dear chap.'

He locked his car then turned back but Drew Grant was still blocking his path. As ever, Robert was maddeningly calm.

'How long do you intend to stand there?'

'Until I get my message across.'

'Aren't you delivering it to the wrong address?' suggested the other. 'Let's face it, Grant. Your argument is with Katie herself, not with me. I'm not the one who rejected you.'

'Shut up!'

'This is private property. Please take yourself off it.'

Drew Grant thrust his face into Robert to emphasize a point.

'Katie does not want you bothering her.'

'Is that what she says?'

'It's what she wants.'

'How do you know?' challenged Robert. 'You haven't spoken to her because she's not receiving calls from anybody. Her father told me that. He also told me how often you've been baying down the line at him. It sounds as if you're the one doing all the bothering.'

'This is a difficult time for her,' said Drew almost reasonably. 'Katie needs to be left in peace. She doesn't want the past dredged up again.'

'Which is exactly why you should steer clear,' countered Robert. *You're* her past. She flushed you

160

away with the rest of the waste matter.'

'Don't push me, Alexander!'

'All I'm saying is this. You had your turn – and failed.'

'At least she got engaged to me.'

'A temporary aberration.'

'We had something special – until you came along.'

'That's a matter of opinion.'

'Then you started your little tricks.'

'I'm sorry, Grant,' said Robert peremptorily, 'but I've had a very busy day and I'm much too tired to listen to you playing the same old record at me again. If Katie wanted you to interfere in her life, she'd ask you. As it is, she chooses to ignore you completely.'

Drew grabbed him by the lapels and pushed him back against the car but Robert Alexander did not suffer such treatment lightly. Dropping his briefcase, he took hold of Drew's wrists and pushed them hard. It was a trial of strength. Drew was taller and fitter but it was the other man who had the greater power. Slowly but surely, he detached the hands from his lapels and forced Drew backwards. A final shove sent the nocturnal visitor back a few paces.

'Goodnight,' said Robert. 'So nice of you to drop by.'

Trembling with fury, Drew Grant pointed a menacing finger.

'If you touch Katie again – I'll kill you!'

He blundered swiftly off into the night.

Eric Fretton skimmed through the article and was partially appeased. Hawker had given him the first in a series about the marriage between Katie Britwell and Mel Edmunds. It was good stuff. Terse, punchy and well-informed. Eric could already see the pictorial content that would accompany the article. His mind was playing around with layout.

'It's good,' he conceded.

'Does that mean I get paid this month?'

161

'You'll have to wait till Val gives me my pocket money.'

'I'm almost there, Eric!'

'As the art mistress said to the gardener.'

They were sharing a lunchtime drink at the wine bar beneath the magazine offices. Eric was working his way steadily through a carafe of Sauternes while Hawker contented himself with a large bitter lemon. The editor read the article again and grunted his approval. He looked up.

'By the way, what did you *do* in Rome?'

'Watch tennis. Search for a killer.'

'Is that all, Hawker?'

'Eh?'

'I saw that look on your face when you got back,' said Eric. 'Talk about the smile before the dick goes in. You been wasting company money on a Continental Nookie tour?'

'The money wasn't wasted.'

'We pay you to write feature articles.'

'They have to be researched in depth.'

'And what have these deep researches told you?'

'Not to use emergency exits in hotels. Not to speak to strange policemen. Not to trust anybody with lots of money.'

'What about the name of the murderer?'

'I've only pencilled that in.'

'Do I get told who it is?'

'After the French Open. I'll be sure then.'

'How do you know?'

'Trust me.'

'Val said that thirty years ago,' he recalled with a shudder. 'I finished up having to marry her six weeks before the twins were born.'

'I'm almost certain,' admitted Hawker. 'There's just one last thing I need to know and it'll clinch it.'

'Extra! Extra! We Name The Guilty Man!'

162

Hawker remained enigmatic. A thought stirred.

'Eric . . . '

'It's your round.'

'Do you remember Alf Tupper?'

'The Tough of the Track? Of course. Great stories.' Nostalgia brought a roseate bloom to his cheeks. 'They don't write stuff like that any more. It was soul-stirring. I mean, it was *literature*!' He gargled with a mouthful of Sauternes before swallowing it. 'Why do you ask?'

'No reason,' said Hawker casually. 'Listen, what's the name of your contact at the ITF?'

'Binkie Morant. Director of Development.'

'How well do you know him?'

'We play golf together,' said the editor. 'You can't know a man better than that. I've seen every mean impulse that man's got. Every dark passion. Every flaw. Golf is not a game – it's a window on the mind.'

'Would he do a favour for you?'

'Owes me dozens.'

'Ask him about one of his colleagues, please.'

'Name?'

'Robert Alexander. Find out all you can. Discreetly.'

'Will do.'

'And ask him if Alexander's been in Paris recently.'

'Why?'

'It's important.'

'I'll remember,' said Eric confidently, then slapped his forehead with the palm of his hand. 'Jesus Christ! I forgot!' He pulled a letter from the pocket of his denim waistcoat. 'This was in this morning's post for you. I knew I had to give you something.'

'You'll never make a carrier pigeon.'

'Pity,' mused the other. 'I think I'd enjoy crapping on pedestrians from three thousand feet. Lot of job satisfaction in that.'

'Mm. France,' noted Hawker, studying the envelope.

'That's what reminded me. You mentioning Paris.'

Hawker slit open the envelope and took out a sheet of expensive stationery. It had an artistic monogram in pink at the top. He read the short note and blinked in surprise.

'Who's it from?' asked Eric.

'Lia Barelli. She wants to see me.'

The pressures on Katie Britwell grew more intense. Refusing to go out, she found the cottage becoming claustrophobic. Wanting to be alone, she could not cope with her own company. Needing to forget, she just kept on remembering. The tragedy was that the people closest to her were the very ones to whom she could not turn. Gerald and Phyllis Britwell were kind and loving parents. But they simply would not understand.

Katie came out of her room and wandered downstairs. Her father was in the garden. Her mother had gone to the village stores. Penny the dog was lapping water from her bowl in the kitchen. Katie flopped down on the sofa in the living room, reached for a magazine, flipped through it, then threw it aside. She crossed to switch on the television and stared at an old gangster film for a few minutes without really seeing it.

Her attention moved to the pile of video cassettes on the shelf. Gerald Britwell liked to record all the gardening programmes. His wife had a fondness for royal occasions. But there was one interest that was mutual and it resulted in over a dozen carefully-preserved cassettes. They had a cherished televisual record of their daughter's career.

Katie willed herself up off the sofa. Moving to the shelf, she selected a video, slipped it into the machine and pressed the start switch. The familiar music played and the opening captions came up on the screen. She kneeled on the carpet only feet away as the Wimbledon

Ladies Singles Final of the previous year began.

Nance Paulson versus Katie Britwell.

It was like watching two complete strangers.

They came out on court to vigorous applause, curtseyed in unison to the royal box then made their way to the chairs either side of the umpire. They knocked up, removed their cardigans, tested their racket strings, had a sip of barley water, took up their positions, waited for the call to start and then sent another championship final winging its way into history. Nance Paulson was playing with her customary power and composure. Katie Britwell seemed nervous and over-eager to please the partisan crowd. Games went with serve until they reached 5-5.

Then Katie played the best tennis of her life.

Increasing her tempo, she put Nance under real pressure, making her run, stretch, guess, take chances. The rallies were long, tense, full of infinite variety. Each point produced an enthralling one-act drama that made the crowd cheer, gasp, sigh and thrill. Both players lifted their game to new heights. Their shots began to defy the laws of geometry. They took each other into a new realm of excellence. It was hypnotic.

Watching it all again now, Katie became caught up in the unique atmosphere of Wimbledon. She sensed the excitement. She felt the adrenalin course. She responded to her devoted following. On the famous centre court at the All-England Club, she had the finest moment of her career. Breaking Nance Paulson's serve with an impossible cross-court passing shot, she held her own to win the first set.

The strongest player in women's tennis was shown to have weaknesses. In those twelve minutes of pure magic, a living legend was cut to size and revealed as a fallible human being. At the most celebrated venue in the game, a British player was restoring national pride and consorting with the immortals of yesteryear.

Now, as then, Katie experienced a sense of joyous release.

Jumping up from the carpet, she ran across to the telephone and started to dial a number. She could bear the accumulated pain no longer.

It was time to face the truth.

Chapter Six

Hawker drove his car as fast as the traffic, a rattling exhaust pipe and his own sense of safety would allow. He hit the country, swung off the main road and began to explore a network of winding lanes. It was early evening by the time he pulled up in front of the cottage. Penny barked a welcome from the other side of the box hedge. Gerald Britwell opened the gate to greet him. Phyllis had tea and pleasantries waiting.

Katie had made efforts. She was wearing a white cotton blouse and a pair of tight-fitting white slacks. Her mules had gold patterning on them. A blue chiffon scarf was tied in her hair and it trailed down to her shoulders. She had taken care with her make-up. The sorrow still showed but it was no longer all-engrossing.

Hawker was pleased to see the improvement in her and even more pleased when she suggested a walk. Katie had been hiding away in the cottage ever since her return. That she should choose to make her first bid to escape in his company was seen as a significant breakthrough by Hawker. Penny volunteered to go with them by wagging her tail but Katie wanted to be alone with her visitor.

They strolled up the main street of the village in pleasant sunshine. Katie acknowledged the occasional greeting but stayed very close to Hawker as if needing to feel his support. They chatted idly until they were clear of the houses. Their steps then took them down a leafy lane whose verges were pummelled by the recent passage of horses. Katie became tense and fell silent. He waited until she was ready.

'Thanks for coming, Don.'

'Thanks for asking me.'

'I've been trying to for days,' she confessed.

'Was it so difficult?' he said.

'Yes.'

'Why?'

'Hard to explain.' She turned to him. 'Anyway, I'm glad you're here now. It gives me a chance to apologize for last time.'

'That was my fault, Katie.'

'You weren't to know.'

'Felt awful about it. Should've kept my big mouth shut.'

'It was a bad time for me,' she said quietly. 'I just couldn't cope. You happened to press the wrong button.'

'Sorry.'

They came to a fork and elected to continue on down a track that was flanked by hedgerows. Country sounds and smells abounded. A herd of Friesian cows snuffled in a nearby field. The rasp of a tractor sounded up ahead of them.

Hawker was determined to let Katie set the pace and choose the agenda. She was the person who could most help him and yet he had not been able to get near her. He did not want to throw away this second chance. It would probably be his last.

Katie suddenly felt the need to talk rapidly.

'The funeral was ghastly,' she said.

'Was it?'

'I just didn't *know* anybody. I mean, not really. Mel's family were always tucked away in the back of his life. We hardly spent any time with them. Yet there I was, standing next to them in church. Daddy and I felt like intruders. We just didn't belong.' She gave a mirthless laugh. 'It was my husband's funeral and I didn't belong. Can you understand that, Don?'

'I think so.'

'It was weird,' she continued. 'I just didn't know what to say to them. It was as if we spoke different languages. I was so relieved when we got on the plane to come back. Daddy was wonderful, of course – he always is – but it was a terrible strain for him. He hasn't been right since the operation and he tires easily.'

They came to a gateway and paused beside it. A few cows looked up with vapid curiosity then went back to their browsing. Katie rested her arms on the top of the gate. Hawker leaned beside the post.

'He talked a lot about you,' she recalled.

'Your father?'

'Yes, Don. You're one of his heroes.'

'And he's one of my dwindling band of fans.'

'He kept going on about those Olympics,' she said. 'I was only a kid at the time but I do vaguely remember it. Two gold medals. The only two for Britain in athletics. Your face was everywhere. You were famous.' A slight pause. 'Then they tried to take your medals off you.'

'Yes, Katie,' he murmured.

'Something to do with a newspaper, wasn't it?'

'That's right.'

'Jeopardizing your amateur status.'

'So they claimed.'

'What exactly happened?'

It was a question that he always avoided because of its painful associations but this time it was different. Katie was trading. Before she could display her wounds, she wanted to see his. She was much more likely to talk about her suffering to a man who had suffered himself.

'It was a storm in the proverbial teacup,' he told her.

'Who was behind it?'

169

'Officialdom. Some trigger-happy know-all with a rule book.'

'We have those in tennis,' she said ruefully.

'I know, Katie,' he agreed. 'But at least your sport has got rid of its hypocrisy. Those ridiculous distinctions between amateur and professional. You've had Open Tennis for over twenty years now and the game has blossomed as a result. Athletics is different.'

'The myth of the amateur.'

'That's how it was in Montreal in 1976. The amateur code was the thing. Nothing must infringe that.' He gazed unseeing across the field. 'I did, Katie. Or, at least, I appeared to do so. A newspaper article was published. How I Won. My name was underneath it. You'd have thought it was the crime of the century! The reaction was unbelievable. I was accused of professionalism and cheating and goodness knows what else. Two days after I'd won my second medal, I had to give both of them back. Suddenly, I was the leper of Montreal.'

'*Did* you write the article?'

'Not really. I gave a long interview to Eric Fretton, that's all. He was covering the Games for a national daily then. Neither of us knew that it would come out as mine.'

'All that fuss over one newspaper article!'

'Exactly,' said Hawker. 'When there were other athletes on drugs and taking backhanders and sneaking all kinds of advantages.'

'But you got your medals back.'

'In the end. The point at issue was whether or not I'd been paid for the article. I hadn't.' He gave a wry smile. 'Eric told me afterwards that if they had paid me, the going rate would have been thirty pounds. Just think, Katie. It took me four years of hard slog to win those medals and I could've lost them for fifteen quid apiece.'

'Why did things get so out of hand?'

'Politics, of course. Karl-Jurgen Voigt won the silver

medal in the 5,000 and the bronze in the 10,000. If I'd been disqualified, he'd have reaped the benefit. Remember that know-all with the rule book?'

'German, by any chance?'

'How did you guess?' he said with a grin.

'East or West?'

'East.'

'They're the worst.'

'Karl-Jurgen was a major in the army, which meant that he was effectively a full-time athlete. A professional in uniform. But *I* was the one who was supposed to have betrayed my amateur status for thirty pieces of silver.'

'Nowadays, athletes can earn a fortune.'

'Yes,' he sighed. 'Hypocrisy works in new ways now. They're still amateurs yet they can rake in thousands. Sponsorship, appearance money, endorsements. They even have their own columns in the papers. It's okay for athletes to earn money as long as they don't actually spend it. The loot goes into a trust fund until they retire from sport. What kind of amateur code is that? When I was running, all we got was travel expenses. I remember hitching a lift up to a meeting in Birmingham once, then feeling guilty because I'd diddled them out of a few quid.'

Katie nodded then came to a quick decision.

'Don . . . '

'Yes?'

'Can we go somewhere?'

'What's wrong with here?'

'Somewhere more private.'

'I'll ask the cows to move further away, if you like.' He saw that she was serious. 'Sure, Katie. Wherever you wish.'

'Let's go for a drive,' she suggested.

'In my old boneshaker? The exhaust rattles.'

'I don't care.'

'Wait till you hear it.'

They strolled back to the cottage and explained the situation. Gerald and Phyllis were pleased. They saw Katie's desire to get away for a bit as a healthy sign. Hawker drove her off. The car behaved itself at a more sedate speed with only a gentle tapping noise from below.

'Where am I going?' he asked.

'Towards London.'

'Much nicer out here.'

'Too nice.'

He did as he was instructed and they chatted about her parents. Katie talked about the health problems which had slowed them both down and how much older they looked each time she went home. They had been totally committed to her career and given what help they could. In that respect, she had no criticism of them.

Hawker felt able to toss in an important question.

'How did they take to Mel?'

'They didn't,' she confessed.

'Oh.'

'They liked him as a person,' she explained. 'He made them laugh and, of course, he was a Wimbledon champion. They idolized him for that. Daddy, especially.' She made a clicking sound with her teeth. 'But they didn't want him as a son-in-law.'

'Did they tell you that?'

'Not in so many words. They wouldn't. Well, you've met them.'

'Sign language?'

'They get their feelings across.'

'And what was their objection to Mel?'

'He was American, for a start!' She gave a short laugh.

'Anything else?'

'Lots of things.' Katie was serious again. 'They just didn't think he was good enough for me. Mummy and

172

Daddy are very sweet but, on the quiet, they're frightful snobs. They didn't trust Mel. They didn't think he was properly educated. They couldn't relate to him. And they were certain the marriage wouldn't last.' Katie rubbed a finger against her side-window. 'They weren't the only ones. Nobody gave Mel and me a hope in hell.'

'Does that include his parents?'

'They were top of the list.'

'I suppose you weren't good enough for their son.'

'No. His mother just told me I was the wrong type.'

'To your face?'

'They believed in getting things out in the open.'

'Must have been tough going.'

'Well, they did become a bit abrasive once or twice but I got used to it. That was Mel's style as well. Shoot from the hip.'

'Why did you marry him?'

Katie stared through the front window of the car as if she had not heard the question. Hawker backed off at once and they travelled in a bruised silence for a couple of miles. She sat up as if coming awake after an unscheduled nap.

'Is there somewhere we can talk, Don?'

'A pub? Restaurant?'

'Away from people, I mean. I'm finding this all rather difficult.' She put a hand on his arm. 'Do you have a place?'

'Flat in Fulham. It's in a dreadful mess.'

'Makes no difference.'

'It's pretty basic.'

'How long will it take us to get there?'

'Let's find out.'

The car accelerated and the exhaust pipe rattled in protest but Hawker kept his right foot firmly down. Katie was ready to unburden herself. He wanted to get her to the place where she could do it. He spent the rest of the journey apologizing for the state of his flat. Katie did her best to lessen his embarrassment.

They got to Fulham, parked the car and went into the house. The flat did have a bomb site feel to it but it improved markedly after Hawker had raced around to tidy it. While he was in the kitchen making coffee, Katie looked around. She noticed the photograph of Elaine then examined all of Hawker's trophies. His athletics career had been both long and successful.

Coffee arrived and they settled down to drink it. Hawker let her take her time. She would not be rushed. She had to feel that the atmosphere was right. They talked generally about sport and Hawker told her about some of his forthcoming commitments for the magazine. As the main feature writer, he had a fairly roving commission that allowed him to explore across a wide spectrum. Tennis was a new field for him. He was finding it very educative.

'Tell me about your wife,' she invited.

'Elaine? She was smashing.'

'How long were you married?'

'Three years.'

'Is that all?'

'We were friends,' he said simply. 'Lovers as well, of course. And colleagues in the athletics team. But – most of all – we were just tremendous friends. People don't seem to understand what I mean by that.'

'I think I do.'

'Elaine was so easy to have around.'

'She looked lovely.' Katie indicated the photograph.

'She was.'

'When was that taken?'

'About six months after we were married.'

Katie put her cup aside and sat on the edge of the sofa. She looked deep into his eyes with an intensity that warned him of what was to come. Hawker braced himself.

'Elaine committed suicide, didn't she?'

'Yes.'

'How?'

He winced. It was a subject he discussed with nobody because it distressed him so much, but he had to overcome his reluctance now. Katie was trading again. An insight into his pain would help her to talk about her own. They were linked by the loss of their marital partner. It was a key that Hawker was forced to use.

'Elaine cut her wrists,' he said flatly.

'Oh, no!'

'She slashed her wrists then went for her throat.'

'Were you the one who found her?'

'Yes. Hours too late.'

'Where?'

'In our bedroom. Saturday afternoon. I'd been out.'

'Oh, Don, I'm so sorry,' said Katie, tears of sympathy forming. 'It must've been soul-destroying.'

'It was. It still is.'

'Why did she do it?'

'I don't know.'

'Wasn't there a note?'

'Nothing. Just Elaine.'

'Had there been any . . . warning signs?'

'No,' said Hawker softly. 'She was a relaxed, easy-going sort of girl. Didn't get uptight at all. We had no big problems. In fact, we'd just put a deposit down on our first home. Elaine had everything to live for – or so I thought.'

Katie took his hands and squeezed them between hers.

'Do you ever regret marrying her?'

'Never!' There was a quiet finality.

'I regretted marrying Mel,' she confessed. 'And I know he had reservations about me. But it was too late by then. We had to make the most of it. Keep up appearances.'

'How soon did you know?'

'Within the first month. It was just a mistake, Don.'

'Then why did you go through with it?'

'Because it seemed like the only way out.'

'Of what?'

Katie bit her lip and brought her hands up to her face. He could see the effort it was costing her to come to terms with it all, and he waited patiently. She shook her head and sighed.

'I'd always liked Mel,' she said. 'He was good fun. As long as you didn't take him too seriously. Over the years, we fell into a kind of nice, friendly, jokey relationship. There was nothing devious about Mel. What you saw was what you got. I liked that.'

'So you were never really close?'

'Hell, no,' she said with dignity. 'I didn't want to end up as just another name in his scrapbook. Plenty of other girls volunteered for that privilege. He didn't need me. Besides, I was engaged to someone else at the time.'

'Drew Grant.'

'He was in right at the start of Katie Britwell.'

'So he told me.'

'Drew was sweet,' she said. 'A real okay guy. Solid as they come – that's why my parents liked him so much. I suppose it was part of the appeal for me as well.'

'In what way?'

'Charging around the world to play tennis soon loses its glamour. You want a home to come back to when you need to recharge the batteries. Someone you can just curl up with. Drew seemed to fit the bill.'

'But it didn't work out.'

'Not for me. Only for him.'

'When did Mel come on the scene?'

'Last May,' she recalled fondly. 'At the French Open, actually. Same old story. I got within three points of beating Nance and blew it. Mel came to see me

176

afterwards and told me that I should have won – as if I didn't know that!'

'What did you say?'

'Some pretty narky things, I guess,' she remembered with a half-smile. 'I asked him how much he charged for coaching lessons. We had a terrific argument about it. A real slanging match.'

'And then?' nudged Hawker.

'He calmed me down and took me off to dinner. Some chic little restaurant in Montmartre.' The half-smile broadened. 'He was right. When I let him say his piece, he was dead right. Mel saw clean through my game. You can imagine how I was feeling after my defeat but he talked me up off the floor. By the end of the meal, I could've pushed a house over.' She gave a helpless shrug. 'Next thing I know, we're back in my room.'

'And that was how it started?'

'Yes – not that I realized it at first.'

'What do you mean?'

'Next morning, I felt so mad with myself,' she admitted. 'I'd vowed and declared it would never happen to me – and yet it did. Mel Edmunds. Superstud. I'd let him. I felt so used.'

'I can understand that.'

'Then Mel bounces back with three dozen red roses and tells me that we're flying off to Bermuda in a few days.' She grinned happily. 'Talk about being swept off my feet. I didn't get chance to say no. Off we went and it was quite wonderful. We played tennis, we lay on the beach, we talked, we got close. It began to seem like the real thing.'

'Were you still engaged to Drew Grant?' he wondered.

'Yes,' she said sadly. 'It was at the terminal stage but I hadn't had the heart to break it off. Once Mel came into my life, I did. We just couldn't see enough of each

177

other and yet we had to keep it all secret. After Wimbledon, we decided to make it public.'

'So you married Mel on the rebound from Drew?'

'There was another person in the frame as well,' she murmured. 'While I was still engaged, I'd had an affair with someone. It got too complicated. I can't explain. The simple fact is that I was all screwed up when Mel waltzed into my life. He was a chance to start fresh. I took it. You know the rest.'

'Your career bloomed and his ran into trouble.'

'He helped me so much on court, Don,' she said. 'I'll always be grateful to him for that. He concentrated so much on my game that he neglected his own.'

'Was that the only reason he started to hit problems?'

'No,' she conceded. 'It was the marriage. We both knew it hadn't worked. I lost myself in tennis, Mel just brooded. He was a free spirit. He should never have got tied down. Know what I'm saying?'

'Marriage emasculated him.'

'Mel had a more colourful phrase but it comes to the same thing.'

'He came good in Monte Carlo,' reminded the other.

'Yes!' she said. 'I'm glad he had that.'

Hawker moved to sit beside her on the sofa.

'Who did you go to see in Paris?' he asked.

Katie shuddered and seemed to be on the point of tears.

'I can't tell you that, Don. Please don't ask again.'

'Okay.'

She thanked him with a kiss on the cheek then rested her head against his chest. Hawker slipped an arm around her shoulders. They stayed together in silent communion for a very long time, each drawing from the other. Eventually, Katie announced her decision.

'I'm going to play in the French Open.'

'That's great news!'

'Mel would've wanted it. This is for him.'

She snuggled down on his chest again and pondered. After a few minutes, she smiled, sat up and looked across at him.

'Would you do a very special favour for me?'

'Anything, Katie.'

Gerald and Phyllis Britwell retired to bed early and soon fell asleep. They had stopped worrying about their daughter. She was in good hands and must be enjoying herself to stay away so long. Her parents slept soundly as a result but their slumber was soon disturbed. A loud creaking noise insinuated itself into their bedroom. Gerald heard it as he opened his eyes. The noise continued then stopped abruptly. It was soon followed by a more identifiable sound.

'What is it?' mumbled Phyllis, stirring.

'I'll go and see, dear.'

'Who's out there?'

'I don't know.'

Clambering out of bed, he padded across the bedroom to the window that overlooked the rear of the cottage. He pulled back the curtain then shielded his eyes against the glare of the floodlight. The tennis court was illuminated and the net had been wound back up.

Gerald was mesmerized. He could not believe what he saw.

Katie was playing tennis with Don Hawker.

She had found herself again.

Dimitri served the drinks while Alain kept up the smalltalk. They were on the verandah of the artist's Monte Carlo villa with a dozen or more guests. There was plenty of bright chatter and tinny laughter. Everyone basked in the hospitality. Jean-Louis Croizier was there with his wife. They knew that there would be a surprise at the party because that was in the nature of

Alain Dupont. A generous man who cared for his friends, he always liked to offer them that little bit extra.

When the party was at its height, he clapped his hands for attention then gave them one of his theatrical bows. Dimitri stood at his side in a loose fitting blue silk shirt with matching trousers and espadrilles. His eyes were watchful behind the mirror sun-glasses.

'Ladies and gentlemen,' began Alain. 'Or lads and lasses, as they say where I come from . . . We have a treat in store for you.'

'Bring on the dancing girls!' called someone.

'In *my* house!' retorted Alain with comical over-reaction.

'So what is this treat?' asked Nance Paulson. 'You gonna buy us *all* a Ferrari?'

Dimitri led the laughter. Alain waved it to an end.

'Follow me – and prepare to be amazed.'

'Keep your trousers on!' pleaded a comedian.

Amusement carried them all the way through to the studio where they fanned out into a semi-circle around the easel. A large canvas stood ready to be unveiled. Taking his place beside it, Alain took hold of the corner of the material. Dimitri slid off to put on a record.

'Friends,' said Alain grandly. 'This is a case of artistic necessity. A portrait that simply *had* to be painted even though its subject was against the idea. Since he refused to co-operate with me, I had to wait until he was in no position to object.'

He flicked his fingers and Dimitri turned on the record. The funeral tones of the Dead March boomed out across the room.

'Behold!' said Alain. 'Nude Reclining!'

He flicked the cloth away from the canvas and gloated over his work. Gasps, grunts and chuckles came from his audience. They were not quite sure what to make of it. Alain Dupont had recreated the murder of Mel Edmunds. Splayed out on the carpet next to the sofa, the American was face down in his own blood, his white bathrobe spattered with red and his head a mass of gore. There was a graphic suddenness about the painting that was too much for some people and they turned away, but Jean-Louis Croizier was delighted with it. A chord had been touched in him.

'*Superbe, Alain!*' he congratulated. 'Is it for sale?'

'Oh, no,' said the artist. 'This one is for *my* collection.'

It was left to the startled Nance to voice a criticism.

'That's in pretty bad taste,' she said with anger. 'Don't you dare let Katie see that!'

The French Open was one of the favourite tournaments in the players' calendar. Wimbledon had more prestige, Flushing Meadow might offer more prize money, and the great, circular edifice in Flinder's Park, Melbourne, might be more astounding with its eggshell green hue, but the Stade Roland Garros had qualities that they could not match. Of the four Grand Slam venues, it was easily the most piquant and flavoursome. Built in Auteuil in 1928 to stage the defence of the Davis Cup, it was magnificently restored in 1980. Fountains, flowers and extended promenades greet the visitor. The competing smells of Gaulois, garlic and steak frites fill the air. Parisian style and excitability add character. And the russet-coloured centre court is an apron stage on which the finest tennis players in the world act out their dramas.

Yuri Chegenyov preferred it to anywhere on the circuit.

'Hello again.'

'Oh, Hi there, Yuri.'

'I hope to meet you here.'

'You're on for a hat trick, aren't you?'

181

'Hat trick?' The Russian's knowledge of English idiom was limited.

'Yes,' said Christina. 'You won in Hamburg and Rome. This would make it three in a row. A hat trick.'

'Ah yes. I like that.'

Christina was giving him that radiant smile again and it revived his hopes. He was talking to her at Roland Garros near the Suzanne Lenglen gate. It was a chance encounter, made all the more satisfying by the absence of Alex Kutsk. The Russian player tried to make up for lost time.

'You watch me at the Foro Italico?'

'Wonderful stuff, Yuri!'

'Thank you, thank you!' he said, beaming.

'You were in the zone.'

'In the where?'

'The zone,' she explained. 'It's just a phrase. It means that you played out of your skin. Oh dear, I don't suppose you know what that means either. You were magnificent, Yuri. Couldn't miss a ball. Guido Barelli had no answer to you.'

'That is good. In the zone. I remember that.' He remembered something else and his face darkened. 'I see you in Rome as well.'

'I know.'

'With a man.'

'I was with lots of men. The other photographers.'

'This man was different. I tell. You dine with him.'

'Ah. Don Hawker.'

'Your husband, maybe?'

'No!' she said with a mild screech.

'Your special friend?'

'Oh, yes. Hawker is certainly that.'

Chegenyov nerved himself to learn the worst.

'Your lover?'

'One of them,' she said airily.

'You have *other* men?'

182

'This is the West,' she told him, patting his shoulder. 'We know how to enjoy ourselves. I'm a woman in a man's profession. I have them all around me. So I learned to choose for myself before I got chosen. That way I get what I want. Like Hawker.'

'It is good?' asked Yuri. 'When you are together?'

'In the zone!'

Christina walked off and left him to marvel at the wonder of Western decadence. Chegenyov now wanted more than just a hat trick.

Car trouble on the way to Heathrow slowed Hawker down and his time was running out when he finally arrived. The telephone call to the office had to be as short as possible. When Eric answered, Hawker gabbled.

'Me. Airport. Rush.'

'What is this?' complained Eric. 'A new language?'

'Alexander. Any info?'

'Stop talking in pidgin fucking English!'

'My plane leaves any minute,' stressed Hawker.

'Okay, okay,' soothed the other. 'I played golf with Binkie and got the lowdown on your pal. All written down on a piece of paper. I'll just try to find it.'

Hawker groaned as he visualized the state of Eric's desk top. It would be like searching for a needle in a haystack.

'Hurry!' he urged. 'Panic!'

'Got it!'

'Fast!'

'Okay,' decided Eric. 'Play it your way. Alexander R. First-rate. Background in city. ITF, six years. Three languages. Excellent tennis. Unmarried. Not gay. Private income. Good to mother.'

'Paris?'

'Two visits. First on April 22.'

'Thought so!' The day of the final in Monte Carlo.

'Second visit. Today. Same plane?'

'Thanks, Eric.'

'Bring me back my story!' howled the editor. 'And come home in one piece, will you? Hawker. Loaf. Use.'

'Cheers!'

Hawker slammed down the receiver and sprinted across the concourse. He caught the plane with only minutes to spare. There was no sign of Robert Alexander aboard but the latter was now a definite factor in Hawker's calculations. Katie's admissions had brought everything into focus. He could start to close in on his quarry now.

When they touched down in Charles de Gaulle Airport, he took a bus to the station and caught the train to the Gare du Nord. A brisk walk soon got him to his *pension* in a backstreet. He stayed long enough to check in, leave his suitcase and study his map of Paris, then he went off in search of a taxi. Fifteen minutes later, he was dropped off outside the Barbizon Palace Hotel.

Lia Barelli was preening herself in its gracious lounge, turning the whole place into a set for a fashion shoot. Dressed in a stunning black suit that hugged her figure, she was sitting in a capacious armchair as if facing the cameras. Her poise was impeccable. It made Hawker feel uncouth and ungainly.

'Mrs Barelli?' he said.

'Ah. Signor Hawker.'

'I did appreciate your letter.'

She allowed him to touch but not shake her hand. As he lowered himself into the chair next to her, she inspected his facial damage. The black eye and the bruises were gone but the scar on his forehead was a livid reminder of Vincente's handiwork. Guilt rustled behind her exquisite maquillage.

'I am sorry,' she said. 'I no understand.'

He realized who had dispatched Vincente on his first errand.

'The score has been evened up since then.'

'Score?'

'Nothing,' he said quickly. 'Thank you for your letter, Mrs Barelli. It meant a lot to me.'

'I want you to know truth.'

Her fractured English would have amused in other circumstances but Hawker did not smile. Lia Barelli knew facts that even Katie could not provide. The beautiful Italian model had to be cossetted.

'Would you like a drink of any kind?' he offered.

'No, signor.'

'Something to eat?'

'I no stay long.'

'Shall we move to somewhere more private?'

'I speak here.'

Hawker could see why. The lounge was set at a right angle to the hotel lobby and it afforded a degree of privacy. Lia Barelli had chosen a seat that was backed by an ornate, gilt-framed mirror so that her reflection would deepen her charisma. It was the ideal venue for her. Hawker could not imagine her beginning her confession by a five-barred gate then completing it in a scruffy two-room flat in Fulham. Midnight tennis under floodlight could certainly be ruled out for her.

'I learn about you,' she began.

'Who from?'

'You man to trust.'

'I hope so.'

'No tell this to anyone,' she warned. 'No tell her.'

'It's a promise.'

Hawker was much more likely to conceal it all from Katie. He did not expect to hear anything which would please the widow of Mel Edmunds. Lia Barelli's testimony would serve another purpose.

'I meet him last year. February. We friends.'

Her conversational style would not have appealed to Eric Fretton.

185

'Mel good. He love me. We meet again.'

'When was all this, Mrs Barelli?'

'February. In Holland. Guido no there.'

It was just as well. As she developed her story in halting phrases, a very different Mel Edmunds began to emerge. They had been staying at the same hotel in Amsterdam and had shared a lift. Mel had been overwhelmed with her and pursued his cause over the next couple of days. Uninterested at first, she was slowly won over by his candour and his charm. What was intended as a fling took them both by surprise to become something far more lasting and resonant.

It was ironic. Mel Edmunds worked his way through dozens of names in his address book. With all his advantages, he could have any woman he chose. His mistake was to fall in love with the one woman who was not available. Lia Barelli was a Catholic who would not even contemplate the annulment of her marriage yet she wanted to share her life with Mel. For his part, he courted her assiduously and flew thousands of miles for a few hours of her company.

The constraints on them were enormous. There was far more pining than passion. The affair came to an end when Guido Barelli found out about it and threatened to set Vincente on the American. For Mel's own safety, Lia ended the relationship. Mel was distraught. He had finally found someone he wanted to marry. He was in a vulnerable state. Katie Britwell came on the scene with her problems. They consoled each other and mistook the surface pleasure for something more.

Mel remained in love with Lia Barelli. Less than a month after the marriage, he was in touch with her. They began to meet. Marriage to Katie was a useful camouflage. It deflected the jealous Guido Barelli. But Mel's commitment to the affair – while now having a wife of his own – entailed the most complex arrangements. Katie had not ruined his tennis. The demands of his secret life did the sabotage.

Hawker was touched. While his sympathy stirred for Katie, he saw Mel Edmunds as a haunted figure, trapped in a doomed love affair, yet capable of great consideration and tenderness. There had been two versions of Mel Edmunds. It was Katie's bad luck to get the inferior version. The other was the property of Lia Barelli.

'You no say,' she insisted. 'All is over now.'

'I can't thank you enough.'

'I go, signor.'

'One last thing, Mrs Barelli . . . '

'Yes?'

'The day of the final in Monte Carlo.'

'Go on.'

'Did Mel ring you that evening?'

'No.'

'Did you expect a call?'

'I hoped,' she said. 'He knew Guido would fly to Rome. I alone in Cannes. He no ring.' Her face tightened. 'He no ring again.'

Hawker thanked her once more. She had told her story with dignity and without shame, anxious to furnish details which might lead, indirectly, to the capture of Mel's killer. As he listened to the account of the love affair, Hawker had a curious thought.

Lia Barelli was the real widow.

She rose to leave and he escorted her out to a taxi. Neither of them noticed the Lamborghini parked on the opposite side of the road. The taxi drove off and Hawker strode away. Inside the car, a newspaper was lowered.

The bandaged head of Vincente was revealed.

Anticipatory delight greeted the start of the French Open. The absence of Mel Edmunds meant that a new men's singles champion would be crowned. The presence of Katie Britwell suggested that the reigning women's singles champion should look to her laurels. It all added spice to the event. Katie herself was investing all her emotional capital in the tournament. Winning the French Open would be a way of repaying Mel and of keeping his memory alive for her. She was back in the city where they had been drawn together. Paris expected.

The city held less fragrant memories for her as well.

'Katie!'

'Oh. Hello, Robert . . .'

'I was hoping to catch you some time.'

'Were you?'

'I saw your first round match. Splendid stuff.'

'Thank you.'

'Nance Paulson must be shaking in her shoes.'

'I doubt it.'

Robert Alexander had intercepted her as she came off court after a practice session. He was excessively polite and courteous to her but he still made her flesh creep. The circumstances of their last meeting hung in the air between them.

'I rang you at home, Katie.'

'I know.'

'You ignored all my calls.'

'I didn't want to speak to anyone.'

'Except the intrepid Mr Hawker.'

'Don is a friend.'

'So am I.'

'Are you?'

She looked at him with mingled hatred and fear. Her desire to strike out at him was tempered by her anxiety over the consequences. He still had a power that could be used against her.

Robert became solemn. 'This is the first opportunity

188

I've had to say how sorry I am about Mel's death. It was a truly distressing business and you have all my sympathy.'

'Sympathy is not your strong point,' she accused.

'That's unfair, Katie.'

'Is it?'

'I merely wanted to offer my condolences.'

'Why? You had no time for Mel.'

'I admired him as a player.'

'You despised him.'

'Katie . . .'

'And he loathed you.'

'Personalities don't come into it.'

'Of course they do.'

'All that is past now.'

'If Mel had ever found out what you did to – '

'He's dead,' said Robert firmly. 'Everything has changed, Katie. The sooner you realize that, the better. You have to make a fresh start.'

Katie was about to walk away but he stepped across to block her path. They had a silent conference for a few moments. A residual fear still kept her burning anger in check.

'I'll be here all week,' he said.

'Will you?'

'At the Hotel Internationale in Neuilly.'

'I see.'

'Could we meet?'

'I'm too busy, Robert.'

'A drink is all that I'm suggesting.'

'That won't be possible.'

'I'm disappointed.'

'Too bad.'

'You know where I am if you change your mind.'

'Goodbye, Robert.'

Emotion showed through at last. He almost pleaded.

189

'Was it really so intolerable, my darling?'

Katie felt her flesh creep all over again.

'Yes,' she said.

High standards and high drama distinguished the matches on the centre court at Roland Garros. Fascinating tactical battles took place on the clay court. The loose, gritty surface robbed the ball of its pace and protracted the rallies. There was no room for the buccaneering style of play that prospered at Wimbledon and Flushing Meadow. Cut-and-thrust tennis was out of place. Patience, cunning and skilled racket-work were at a premium. Stamina was vital. It was a tournament for stayers.

Hawker watched Nance Paulson eliminate Laura Lennig. As he left the Press Box, a military figure strode over to him. The voice alone was enough to set Hawker's teeth on edge.

'Still hanging around, are we?' said Quentin Rivers.

'Yes.'

'Haven't you had enough yet, Hawker?'

'Of what?'

'Wasting your time, old boy.' Rivers was charmingly derisive. 'We all know that you were a fine athlete two hundred years ago, but sportswriting is too important an art to be left to sportsmen. It needs the well-informed expert with a literary turn of mind.'

'Then how come you're in it, Rivers?'

'Read my articles and you'll find out.'

'No, thanks.'

'Robert Alexander tells me you've been bothering him as well.'

'When did he tell you?' asked Hawker. 'Over a pint of blood at the club?'

'Very droll, Hawker.'

'I won't keep you.'

'Robert intimated something quite extraordinary to me.'

'His turn to scratch *your* back?'

'This concerns you, old boy,' said Rivers in mocking tones. 'After that strange behaviour of yours at the ITF offices, Robert got hold of the notion that you're actually trying to solve the mystery of Mel Edmund's murder.' Rivers chuckled. 'What makes you think you can succeed where the police have failed?'

'I look in the right places.'

'Alf Tupper rides again!'

'That joke is wearing a bit thin.'

'It still raises a snigger in the Press Room.'

'And the club.'

Rivers glowered and stepped in closer to him.

'People like you sicken me, Hawker.'

'Good.'

'Moral crusaders who are never happy unless they're waving some damn banner about. This time it's "Justice for Mel Edmunds". Utter nonsense! What does it matter *who* killed the fellow? Mel Edmunds was an excrescence. A wart on the face of tennis. Quite frankly, I think we're better off without him.'

'It's easy to attack a man when he can't defend himself.'

'Mel did *his* share of attacking when he was alive.'

'How come?'

'Ask Robert Alexander.'

'I'm asking you.'

'He gave *me* some stick. Had the temerity to disagree with an article I'd written about him. Said I was a scumball.'

'I think he was trying to flatter you.'

Quentin Rivers bridled and struck back immediately but his barbs had no effect on Hawker. The latter was not listening. His attention had been diverted by someone behind Rivers' shoulder. Higher up the stand

191

was a tall, spare man with a shock of red hair.

It was Drew Grant.

Yuri Chegenyov sat in the dining room at the Russian Embassy and let his hosts heap their praises upon him. Alex Kutsk was luxuriating in it all but the player was becoming increasingly restive. They were in a large, elegant dining room around a long table. Framed portraits of Soviet leaders lined the walls. The meal had been prepared by a Russian chef. Vodka had been specially imported. The talk revolved around the political scene in Moscow. Tennis was an adjunct.

Chegenyov looked around in mild disgust. He was in one of the most exciting and sensual cities in the world and he was listening to a lot of old men discussing *glasnost*. Nominally in Paris, he was still imprisoned in Moscow. Wherever he went, it was always the same. No fraternization. No friendships. No fun.

He thought about Christina Erikkson's refreshing attitude.

It inspired him.

'Will you win the final, Comrade?' asked the ambassador.

'I will win,' said Chegenyov.

But he was not talking about tennis.

Robert Alexander had official business while he was in Paris but his main reason for being there was to be close to Katie. She had been cold and uncommunicative so far but that was only to be expected. Mel's death was still a recent event. She would need time to get over it properly. Then she would be more approachable. Robert would be able to apply his subtle pressures once more.

Seated at the writing table in his room, he put Katie from his mind to concentrate on the report he was writing. He was soon absorbed in the fine detail of his argument. A knock on the door surprised him. It was mid-evening and he was not expecting a caller. He opened the door with curiosity.

The smiling face of Don Hawker greeted him.

'I thought we might have a little chat, Mr Alexander.'

'We've exhausted all we have to say to each other.'

'May I come in a moment?'

'It's not convenient.'

'Then I'll wait here until it is.'

Robert sighed then relented. He stood aside.

'Five minutes,' he stipulated. 'Then out you go. I have work to do, Mr Hawker.'

'It's about your work that I've come,' said the other, walking into the room. 'Discovered an odd coincidence.'

Robert closed the door and stayed close to it.

'Keep talking,' he encouraged.

'April 22 of this year . . . '

'What about it?'

'You were in Paris that day.'

'Was I?'

'According to my sources.'

'Sources?'

'You have your club: I have my grapevine.'

Robert masked his discomfort behind a noncommittal shrug.

'Supposing I *was* in Paris that day?'

'Katie was here as well.'

'So were millions of other people.'

'I think she came to see you.'

'Is that what Katie says?'

'No,' conceded Hawker. 'For some reason, she can't bear to talk about you. I'm beginning to understand why.'

Robert strolled over to him with his assurance intact.

'I came to Paris that day for a meeting with the

President of the ITF. We had business to discuss. Feel free to confirm that with him.'

'Katie was here because you told her to come.'

'Did I?'

'You rang her at Nance Paulson's house the previous evening.'

'Does your grapevine have phone-tapping facilities?'

'You forced her to come here, didn't you?'

'I'm afraid you've overstayed your welcome.'

'Now I know how.'

Robert stepped across to the telephone and lifted it. When he got through to reception, he spoke in fluent French. The receiver was then replaced.

'No need to order room service on my account,' said Hawker.

'I told them I had an unwanted visitor who wouldn't leave my room. They're sending some security men up.'

'Do I frighten you?'

'No. But you do bore me.'

Hawker advanced on him. 'What are you up to, eh?'

'I might ask the same question of you.'

'What's your game, Alexander?'

'Consult your grapevine.'

'Katie means a lot to me.'

'And to me,' returned the other with subdued feeling. 'I can promise you that I have her best interests at heart.'

'Then why are you blackmailing her?'

'Is that what I'm supposed to be doing?'

His equanimity was impregnable. Hawker resumed the attack.

'Katie told me how she came to marry Mel. She mentioned an affair in her past. I think it was with you.'

'Do you now?'

'She cast you aside before you were ready to go. So

194

you clung on. Even when she was married, she couldn't shake you off.' Hawker confronted him. '*Why*, Alexander? What's the hold you have over her?'

'This is getting very tedious, you know.'

'Then let me put it more bluntly. As of now, you keep clear of Katie. For good. Understand?'

'No, I don't.'

'You're out of the frame. Back off.'

'I make my own decisions about whom I see.'

'Bother her again – and you answer to me.'

'I'm shaking in my shoes, Mr Hawker,' said the other with an educated sneer. 'What are you trying to do? Justify your nickname as the Tough of the Track?'

'Don't push your luck, Alexander.'

'If I wish to speak with Katie – or with anyone else for that matter – I'll do so. There's nothing you can do to stop me.'

'Isn't there?' said Hawker. 'Try this on account.'

He threw a punch which connected with the other's chin and sent him sprawling. Robert fell heavily and grunted with sheer indignation.

There was a banging on the door as security men arrived.

Robert Alexander looked up with malevolence.

'I think it's time for you to go,' he said.

Guido Barelli sat in the corner of the restaurant and helped himself to another glass of Chianti. It had been a bad day for him. The clay court had neutralized his *blitzkreig* tactics and he had suffered an ignominious defeat at the hands of Lars Holmgren. A telephone call to Rome in search of consolation had produced the news that Francesca had landed a part in a film and would be away in Morocco for six weeks. Then he had to face the latest rankings from the ATP computer. Barelli had dropped three places and was out of the top ten. It was a savage blow to his pride.

Finally, there was Lia. The ultimate sorrow.

Estrangements were nothing new in the Barelli marriage. It had always been a tempestuous relationship but the rows were quickly followed by ecstatic reconciliations and their differences were forgotten in a fever of exchanged promises. Lia was refusing even to see him this time. Staying in Paris herself for a series of fashion shows, she had rebuffed all his blandishments. It was a new experience for him and it was not one that he relished.

Only now that she was gone did Barelli appreciate his wife's true value. She was not just a beautiful accessory to his image as one of Italy's greatest sporting stars. She lent him status. When he was with Lia, the cameras were always in pursuit of candid shots of them. His talents kept him on the sports pages but it was his wife who got him to a much wider audience through the gossip columns and the magazines. Without her, he lost some of his credibility.

Mel Edmunds was to blame. Until he entered Lia's life, the marriage had worked to Barelli's advantage. He could play the devoted husband when he was with her and recapture his bachelor freedom when they were apart. It was the best of both worlds. Mel Edmunds had ruined it all. Even after his death, he came between husband and wife.

Barelli thought of the taunts that Hawker had hurled at him in Rome. They stung afresh. Finishing his drink, he got up and headed for the bar. Hawker was the new target. There was payment to exact from him. Not only was he a living reminder of Mel Edmunds, he had been seen at the Hotel Barbizon in lengthy conference with Lia. That had wounded Barelli deeply.

Vincente was perched on a bar stool, overflowing its inadequate surface. Sipping a glass of Pernod, he was studying an Italian newspaper with a glazed interest.

196

The stitches had now been removed from his head but he retained the bandaging to hide the ugly scars.

He glanced up expectantly as Barelli came over to him.

'Vincente . . .'

'*Sì?*'

'When the tournament is over – he is all yours.'

A dark smile spread its way across the big man's face.

It was pleasant to chat to Drew Grant again. Katie had been steadfastly avoiding him and fearing a lot of embarrassment but their meeting at the hotel had been a relaxed and enjoyable one. It was like finding a friend again after an enforced absence. Drew was delighted that she was playing in the tournament and most of his remarks had been geared towards the problem of how to beat Nance Paulson. It was just like it had been in the early days, a comfortable partnership, coach and player bonded together by a common purpose and borne along by a mutual passion for the game.

Katie felt an upsurge of affection for him.

'Thanks for coming, Drew.'

'I wouldn't miss it for the world. Historic occasion.'

'Is it?'

'Nance Paulson about to be toppled in the French Open.'

'It hasn't happened yet,' she reminded.

'It will.'

They were sitting at a table in a pavement cafe not far from her hotel. The warm night air enfolded them and the magic of Paris touched their hearts. Drew paid for the meal and they got up to stroll back. Katie slipped her hand into his as they sauntered along. Drew was what he had always been. A wonderful friend.

When they reached the hotel, she turned to face him

and kissed him lightly on the lips. He squeezed her hands and gazed lovingly at her. Katie enjoyed the moment. It was good to feel such closeness to someone else again. She was calm, soothed, untroubled.

His question caught her completely off guard.

'Katie, was there ever anything between you and Robert Alexander?'

The truth came out before she could hold it in.

'Yes,' she admitted. 'He raped me.'

It was the familiar dream with a few slight variations. Hawker came into the bedroom to find Elaine stretched out on the bed. Her life-blood had drained away and stained the white sheets with sensational effect. He rushed to bend over her and take her in his arms. Then the police came bursting in through the door.

Something dragged Hawker out of his sleep and the nightmare continued in reality. All the elements were there. Bed. Dead body. Blood. Police. It was terrifying.

'M'sieur! Open the door, please!'

Guilt and panic made him sit up in bed with a start.

'Police, M'sieur! Open the door!'

Hawker was sufficiently awake to take his bearings. He was lying naked beside Christina at his *pension*. Far from being dead, she was complaining at the disturbance. The blood he had felt on him was the running sweat of his fear.

What was real was the pounding of the fist on the door.

'M'sieur! Wake up, please!'

'I'm coming!' he called.

'What the hell's going on?' asked Christina drowsily.

'I'll handle it,' he said.

Climbing out of bed, he pulled on a pair of trousers and opened the door. He gaped. In the half-light on the landing, he saw the grim face of Sergeant Raoul

198

Chabrier. A uniformed gendarme was in attendance.

The detective was in brusque mood.

'Come with us, please, M'sieur.'

'Why?'

'You visit L'Hotel Internationale this evening?'

'Yes. I went to see Robert Alexander.'

Chabrier glanced over his shoulder at the sight of Christina sitting up in bed, then his gimlet eyes went back to Hawker.

'M'sieur Alexander has been murdered.'

Chapter Seven

It was almost dawn before they had finished with him. Hawker was locked in a small, airless room with three senior detectives from the French police. They were specialists in homicide. Skilled interrogators of suspects like himself. They knew how to combine charm with intimidation. They insinuated their way into his mind and took away information he had no intention of giving them. He admitted the row, the anger, the punch. He told them of his visit to ITF offices in London.

Hawker was carefully pummelled into exhaustion. It was like playing tennis against three simultaneous opponents, each of whom was markedly superior. Wherever he hit the ball, there was a racket waiting. Whenever his concentration wavered, the ball zoomed back at him from a new direction. No matter what he did, he could not score a point.

Inspector Claude Fournier took his two colleagues aside for a brief discussion in French. They left the room and the bald, portly detective brought Hawker's misery to an end.

'You may leave, M'sieur.'

'Thank God for that.'

'We may need to speak to you again.' It sounded ominous.

'You'll find me asleep somewhere,' yawned Hawker.

'*Au revoir, M'sieur.*'

'Sweet dreams!'

Hawker came out into a corridor and headed for the exit. Two familiar figures appeared ahead of him to block his path. Chief Inspector Yves Daninos looked very sprightly for the time of morning. Sergeant Raoul Chabrier had an owlish stillness. Hawker quailed. Softened up by the French police, he was not ready for further questioning.

'*Bonjour, M'sieur!*' greeted Daninos cheerily.

'Aren't you a bit off your patch?' asked Hawker.

'Our investigations have moved outside the boundaries of Monaco,' explained Daninos. 'We have pursued our enquiries in Hamburg, Rome, London, Washington and New York. Now it is the turn of Paris. We like to work with our French colleagues. They understand our ways.'

'Brothers under the skin.'

'Quite, M'sieur,' said the other. 'Inspector Fournier is an old friend of mine. That is why I felt able to ask for that favour. I hope you appreciated my consideration.'

'Consideration?'

'Yes. I asked Claude to have you brought from the hotel by Raoul here.' A faintly teasing note sounded. 'An English visitor might be upset if he was roused by a strange policeman in the middle of the night. You were no doubt reassured to see that it was Raoul.'

'Very reassured!' said Hawker.

Chabrier gave him a granite stare of disapproval.

Daninos wagged a professorial finger at an erring student.

'You do not have much luck in hotel bedrooms, do you?' he observed. 'Unless Madamoiselle Erikkson is in them with you.'

'I still don't know what happened,' protested Hawker.

'We will tell you on the way back.'

'Where?'

'To our hotel. The car is waiting.'

201

Hawker did not know whether to be pleased or alarmed and so he compromised with a relaxed wariness. Chabrier got into the driving seat of a slate-grey Peugeot. The other two men sat in the back. All three cruised off into the new day that was dawning over the city.

Daninos summarized events. Robert Alexander had worked late at his hotel and rung for supper to be brought up. When the waiter arrived, he got no response to persistent knocking so he let himself in. Robert was lying on his back on the carpet. The front of his skull had been smashed in. No murder weapon was found.

'You can see why we take such interest in the case,' said the Chief Inspector. 'Two dead bodies. One murderer.'

'Not necessarily,' argued Hawker.

'I *saw* M'sieur Alexander.'

'Oh.'

It at least ruled out Hawker's earlier theory that Robert Alexander had in fact been Mel's killer. The second victim narrowed the field considerably. There were dozens of people who had wished Mel Edmunds dead and the original list of suspects was long. Robert was altogether different. A highly successful tennis administrator, respected by all and liked by most. Something of a workaholic, his social life was low-key.

Daninos seemed to read Hawker's mind. He smiled.

'I ask myself the same question, M'sieur.'

'Eh?'

'Who stood to gain most from this man's death?'

Hawker knew the answer at once and it jolted him.

Katie Britwell.

The murder cast a blight over the championships and introduced an unwelcome note of anxiety. Players and officials became edgy. Two victims so far on the circuit.

Who would be the third? Security was increased and individuals became much more vigilant. The President of the International Tennis Federation was Jacques Cavaille and he did all he could to speed up investigations in his native city. Police activity was intense. Scores of people from the tennis fraternity had to give statements. It made for an unsettled air.

The French Open was not merely a tennis tournament. It was one of the premier events in the Parisian social calendar. The rich and famous – and those aspiring to such dual eminence – flocked to Roland Garros to see and to be seen. Luminaries packed the private boxes near the courtside. Each day brought a spontaneous fashion show as the latest creations by Dior, Yves Saint Laurent, Chanel, Emanuel Ungaro and the dazzling Christian Lacroix went on show. There was a throbbing sensuality about the whole scene.

Beyond the stadium itself, on the grounds adjacent to the courts, was a trade exhibition of the highest quality. The green and white tents of rival enterprises supplied colour, interest and cloying hospitality. Crowds spilled out of matches and into cocktail parties. It was a gigantic commercial jamboree that lent an extra dimension. During the French Open – inside or outside the stadium – there was always plenty to look at.

Nance Paulson found some of her commitments tiresome. In addition to having to battle her way through the stronger half of the draw, she was required to appear in the Bellecroix marquee from time to time, to mix and to market. Jean-Louis Croizier was always in the background, stage managing it all with practised ease striking the proper balance between the social and the commercial. His wife's endorsement of the Belle-croix range had made it the best-selling tennis wear for ladies. But she had to put in the work.

Nance was grateful when another stint ended.

'My God!' she gasped. 'This is worse than playing three sets.'

'You can rest at the hotel, *ma chère*,' promised her husband, while offering his brightest smile to passing acquaintances. 'We have done well today. Our presentation is direct yet sophisticated. Ours is easily the most popular display.'

'As long as it keeps the big bucks rolling in,' she said.

'Of course.'

'That's the name of the game, sweetie.'

'Smile,' he whispered. 'Camera.'

He kissed her fondly on the cheek in time to be photographed for a spread on the tournament in *Paris Match*. Jean-Louis always knew when a camera was in the vicinity. It was uncanny.

Alain Dupont and Dimitri swooped down on them.

'It gets better every year!' gushed Alain. 'I've never *seen* so many dear, dear boys. It's an *embarras du choix* and I love it!'

'Have you managed to see any tennis?' joked Nance.

'There's *tennis* as well, darling?' he said in mock wonder.

He twirled around to let them see the outrageous costume that he was wearing. It was a voluminous pink jumpsuit with a jabot at the neck and frills both at the wrists and ankles. A pink straw boater, set at a rakish angle, ensured that nobody would miss him in a crowd. Dimitri was into a red phase. He wore a red silk shirt with puff sleeves above silk pants in a darker hue that tapered down to deep crimson shoes. As he strutted and posed, there was a touch of the bullfighter about him.

Alain looked over at the giant display racket that hung above the Bellecroix collection. Its head was several times larger than a normal racket and its steel shaft was as thick as a net-post.

'Maybe you should borrow that one, Nance,' he suggested.

'I wouldn't have the strength to lift it,' she said.

'Pity. You'll need some superior armoury against Katie.'

'Nance is her own superior armoury,' said Jean-Louis loyally.

'Did you see what Katie did to Ingrid the Bell?' Alain pulled a face. 'My dears, she annihilated the poor creature. Ingrid got one point and that was an unforced error from Katie.'

'Boy!' said Nance. 'You sure know how to build my confidence.'

There was a laugh in her voice but she was decidedly peeved. As fans milled around with programmes, she graciously supplied her autograph and lapped up their admiration.

Jean-Louis took the chance to upbraid his friend.

'That was not very tactful, Alain,' he scolded.

'It wasn't meant to be tactful – just honest.'

'Don't you know that you never praise one woman in front of another?' he asked. 'And you certainly don't praise one tennis player in front of another. It is not just bad manners. It is cruel.'

'Cruel to be kind, dear,' argued the other. 'Nance needs to be tipped off, that's all. Forewarned is forearmed.' He smirked. 'Yes, and she'll need four arms if she's to beat Katie Britwell.'

'Nance will win.'

'Maybe, Jean-Louis.'

'No woman can beat her when it really matters.'

'That's what I thought until I saw Katie today,' said Alain. 'Something's happened to that girl overnight. She was inspirational. She made Ingrid the Bell look pedestrian.'

'Nance will still win.'

'I'll go for Katie.'

'What happened to friendship, Alain?'

'Oh, I adore Nance and always will,' soothed the artist. 'I have supported her loyally for years and never been disappointed. But I'm British, remember. Katie brings out my Yorkshire roots. I'll be there for the final, waving my Union Jack.'

'Nance will be too strong for her.'

'I wouldn't bet on it, dear.'

'She always beats Katie in the big tournaments.'

'I say no more.'

But Jean-Louis Croizier would not let the matter rest. All too conscious of the truth in what Alain was saying, he sought to suffocate it beneath a blanket of assertions that shaded into wild boasts. It was most untypical of him to be so outspoken.

'Nance will win because she *has* to win.' He waved an arm in a circular gesture. 'All this revolves around her. Nance is a megastar. The only megastar in the women's game. That is why Bellecroix got where it did. And why it will stay there.'

'We shall see.'

'Nance will take that title,' said her husband with a hint of menace. 'I will make sure that she does.'

The men's tournament was a succession of complete surprises. Some established stars fell, some unknowns rose, and some seasoned losers suddenly began to string wins together. It made for continuing interest. With Barelli gone, everyone predicted a final between Holmgren and Chegenyov but the biggest shock of the tournament altered that. The Russian went down in a five-set marathon to Jimmy Zapata of Brazil. What was perhaps even more amazing was that Chegenyov did not seem to mind in the least.

'He was better,' he conceded. 'It was that simple.'

'But nine times out of ten, you'd destroy him,' said Christina.

'That is tennis.'

'Don't look so happy about it!'

'But I feel happy,' he said, holding his arms out. 'Instead of being stuck on the practice court getting ready for the final, I can stand in the sun and talk to you.'

They were enjoying a moment together on the empty centre court. Christina had come in early to take some wide-angle shots of the stadium. Chegenyov had brought her to the one place where he would be certain of a measure of privacy. At the very heart of Roland Garros. It was an evocative sight. They imbibed its wonder for a while, strolling around the court itself then gazing up at the banked stands that could hold over 15,000 spectators and which could become avenues of passion and delight during a thrilling match.

'Don't the crowds ever put you off?' she asked.

'I learn to use them.'

'Yes, I've seen you.'

'What else you see?'

'Lots of nice things.'

He smiled and came to stand next to her. He seemed to be winding himself up to make some kind of declaration and Christina prepared to deflect him. But his announcement was not at all what she expected.

'I want to thank you, Christina.'

'For what?'

'All your help.'

'I did nothing,' she said.

'It's not what you did,' he mumbled. 'What you are.'

Here it comes, she thought. Get ready. Let him down gently.

'I have to go away.'

'Back to Russia?'

'Just away. It doesn't matter where.'

'When will I see you again, Yuri?'

'One day.' He scratched the clay surface of the court with one foot. 'I not able to find right words, Christina, but . . .'

'I know, Yuri,' she said.

'Very lucky man. Don Hawker.'

'That's what I keep telling him.'

'Not as lucky as Yuri Chegenyov.'

'Oh?'

'You give me much more.'

'Did I?'

'This!'

He spun round on his heel and his gesture took in the whole stadium. Instead of the pounce she feared, Christina got a chaste kiss on the hand before he walked off jauntily to the exit.

She shook her head in bewilderment and looked around.

'I gave him *this*?'

Hawker noticed the change immediately. It was in her eye, her lip, the tilt of her chin. It was in her bounce and sparkle and new-found confidence. Long before she got near the stadium, he knew that her game would prosper. Katie Britwell had been subdued by one gruesome murder and liberated by another. She had been through a long dark night of the soul then found herself in blazing sunshine. It was heartening to behold and Hawker took full pleasure from it but he knew there were reasons for it all and he waited for an opportunity to find out what they were.

It came that evening at the hotel. When he used the house telephone to say that he was there, she invited him up to her room. It was the first of a number of shocks. The old brooding Katie had gone and a new one took her place, honest, straightforward, positive.

She ushered him to a chair and sat opposite. Dressed for dinner in a becoming lightweight cotton suit, she looked him in the eye and sprung the first surprise.

'I've been holding out on you, Don.'

'Have you?'

'I've been giving you lies, evasions, excuses.'

'All the time?'

'No,' she corrected. 'There were some facts in there but not the ones that mattered. Not the big facts.'

'And what are they?' he asked evenly.

Her eyelids lowered. She played with her fingers.

'Don . . . .'

'Take your time. There's no hurry.'

'If I tell you everything . . . '

'It stays between you and me, Katie. You know that.'

She searched his face and found the confirmation she needed.

'I came to Paris that day to see Robert,' she confessed. 'He rang me during dinner at Nance's house. He'd tried the hotel and was told I had gone out for dinner. He rang several restaurants before he got hold of the idea I might be with Nance and Jean-Louis.'

'Persistent.'

'You don't know half of it.'

'What did he want?'

'To see me.'

'On the day of Mel's final?'

'He'd worked out that I could be back in time for that,' she said. 'And I would've been if the flight hadn't been delayed. The simple fact is – I *had* to go to Paris.'

'Why?'

'Oh, it would take an age to explain and you still wouldn't understand all the complications. I'm not sure I do. All I know is that it was hell, Don. Absolute hell.'

She took time to get up strength to go on. Her earlier confidence was waning now and she was speaking more slowly and warily.

'I met Robert some years ago,' she said. 'He was wonderful at first. Kind, friendly, helpful. And very knowledgeable about tennis. He could talk for hours on end about it. We saw each other every now and again. A chat, maybe a drink, never anything more. I mean, I just didn't *think* about him in that way, honestly.'

'But that's how he thought about you,' suggested Hawker.

'Yes,' she agreed. 'Not that he said anything. Years went by and he was still the same man I'd known at the start.'

'What changed him?'

'My engagement to Drew.'

'Ah.'

'Robert had persuaded himself that one day – no matter how long he had to wait – he and I would . . .' She gave a laugh of sudden desperation. 'It was ridiculous. He was having this grand love affair with me and I didn't know a thing about it!'

'Until you became Drew's fiancée.'

'That really got to Robert,' she recalled. 'Not just that I'd betrayed him and chosen someone else. But that the someone else was Drew Grant. The two of them hated each other.'

'Chalk and cheese.'

'Anyway, that's when it all began.'

'Drew told me about the way he persecuted you.'

'It was unbelievable, Don,' she said. 'I didn't dare to tell Drew some of the things that went on. Robert followed me. Like a bloodhound sniffing my trail. He'd turn up in New York, Berlin, Prague, even Tokyo on one occasion. Always pretending he had to be there on behalf of the ITF – which was true sometimes – but chasing me really.'

'I know that Drew tried to scare him off.'

'That only made it worse. Robert became more careful.'

'In what way?'

'He trailed me without my even knowing it.' Her voice dwindled to the merest whisper. 'He saw something he shouldn't have seen.'

A stab of pain made her catch her breath and she clenched her fists tight. Hawker got to his feet and hurried to the bathroom, returning with a glass of cold water. Katie took it gratefully and sipped. Hawker sat on the floor beside her.

The words now trickled out with painful slowness.

'He . . . threatened . . . to tell . . . '

'Who?'

'He . . . cornered me . . . badgered . . . me . . . '

'Was he going to tell Drew?'

Katie shook her head. 'Worse than that.'

He wanted to ask her what she meant but Katie had drifted off into a kind of trance now. All he could do was to stay there and listen. She would only tell him when she felt ready.

'That's when Mel came along,' she remembered. 'I was in a hopeless position by then. Engaged to Drew but not wanting to marry him. Threatened by Robert. My game cracking up. Mel seemed like the answer to a prayer. I thought it would solve all my problems.'

'Only Robert wouldn't give up, would he?'

'It was worse than ever, Don. You know what his opinion of Mel was. He felt I'd kicked him in the teeth on purpose. Some of the phone calls I had . . . they turned my stomach.' She emptied the glass. 'I managed to dodge him for months, changing my plans at the last moment, dropping out of tournaments and so on. But it couldn't last.'

'You came to Monte Carlo.'

'Robert made his move,' she said wearily. 'He warned me that, if I didn't go to Paris to see him that morning, he'd . . . he'd tell my husband and tell my parents.'

'About this other affair you'd had?' he asked gently.

211

'Yes. I was trapped Don. I felt it was the only way out. If I gave him what he wanted, he'd go away and leave me alone. So I flew here from Nice that morning.' She shook her head in disbelief. 'He raped me, Don. I don't mean that he attacked me or used force but that's what it was. A rape. I just lay there helplessly without making a sound while this man used me. I felt so dirty and ashamed. Robert tried to make me say how much I'd enjoyed it but I couldn't. It was an ordeal.' She looked at him with eyes brimful of tears. 'I couldn't let him tell my parents. You've met them. They just wouldn't know how to cope.'

'Why not? Who was the person?'

'Someone on the tennis circuit.'

'These things happen all the time,' he argued. 'It's no big deal. Your parents must accept that, surely. Why all the secrecy? Was it someone famous? Chegenyov? Holmgren? Barelli even?'

'I can't tell you the name, Don, and I don't want to say any more. Except one thing. If you promise me we can go straight downstairs for dinner afterwards.'

'Of course, Katie. Whatever you say.'

'The person I had the affair with wasn't a man at all,' she said bravely. 'It was a woman.'

Drew Grant did not neglect his own fitness while he was in Paris. He had brought his rackets and soon found a partner with whom he could play. They repaired to a club not far from Roland Garros and had their own version of the Men's Singles Final. Drew felt happier than he had done for a long time. Like Katie, he had a sense of escape from a huge burden he had been carrying. His game got the benefit and his opponent took the punishment.

They were about to leave the court when a large Citroen pulled up outside the club. Two men came in through the entrance, looked around the courts then

212

headed for theirs. The portly, bald-headed man took something from his pocket. Approaching Drew, he showed him his identification.

'Inspector Fournier. Criminal Division.'

'Oh.' Drew looked resigned.

'We'd like to ask you a few questions, M'sieur . . . '

Stung by all the media attention being showered on Katie, Nance Paulson went into her semi-final with renewed determination. Sara Clarino could only detain her on court for thirty-nine minutes. Katie herself had a much tougher match against the resourceful Jody Beecher who thrived on the Parisian clay. The match went to three sets before Katie edged it in a tie-break. It had been a titanic struggle and both girls were on the verge of collapse. The advantage shifted back to Nance. An easier semi, more time to recover, the opportunity to watch her opponent in a long testing match. Katie Britwell was no longer the favourite. It was seen as a stalemate. Fifty-fifty.

The crowds descended on Roland Garros on Finals Day with sophisticated eagerness. A dull sky did not depress the spirits. The stands filled, the excitement built, the tension got to the players waiting in the locker room.

Hawker was once again astonished to see Daninos at a tennis tournament. Chabrier was with him and the prospect of an enthralling afternoon had robbed him of his usual lugubrious manner.

Hawker pushed his way across to have a brief word.

'Welcome to a real art form, Chief Inspector.'

'Why, M'sieur? Is Pavarotti playing?'

'No,' said Hawker drily, 'but you can see Placido Domingo and Kiri Te Kanawa in the mixed doubles.'

'*Touché*!' congratulated Daninos.

Chabrier had his first rich chuckle for weeks.

'Is it true that Drew Grant has been arrested?' said Hawker.

'He is helping the police, that is all.'

'When will he be released?'

'When Claude Fournier decides.' A mischievous smile played around the Chief Inspector's lips and he beckoned Hawker closer. 'I can give you some highly confidential information that might interest you, M'sieur. For your ears only.'

'Fair enough. What's the news!'

'Yuri Chegenyov is in police custody.'

Daninos enjoyed the look of utter amazement on Hawker's face.

Guido Barelli and Vincente took up their positions in the players' box. The player savoured the adulation of fans in some nearby seats and bared his teeth in a grin as wide as the Mediterranean when the photographers targeted him. That grin vanished into extinction when he noticed someone in the private box opposite. Surrounded by adoring friends from the fashion world, Lia Barelli wore a striking outfit in royal blue with a large jewelled cross on its front. It did not induce any spiritual feelings in Barelli. He scowled like an apostate during a Papal visit. Lia saw him only to look through him.

A nudge from Vincente switched his gaze to the Press Box. Don Hawker was taking his seat among the tennis writers of the world. It gave Barelli something else to think about.

He would take out his bad temper on Hawker.

'Today, Vincente,' he ordered.

'*Si.*'

'Make it good.'

The bodyguard had been thinking about nothing else.

*

Alain Dupont was part of an artists' colony. The private box with the superb courtside view was filled with a motley collection of painters and sculptors. Tennis was incidental to most of them. They were there for the experience. Competing with each other for outlandish garb, they had to award the palm to Alain. He was wearing his Prince of Denmark costume, a wide-necked white shirt beneath a black doublet and hose. The plunge of his shirt almost reached his navel but a diamond pendant obscured any indecency.

Lars Holmgren of Sweden and Vic Rembrandt of America were the finalists in the Men's Singles. Alain had no patriotic commitments there. It would be different when the ladies took the court. Katie Britwell versus Nance Paulson. The artist would support the country from which he was exiled.

Yorkshire would come to Roland Garros.

Alf Bridge would revert to type for the match.

Jean-Louis Croizier was shown into a room at the back of the reception counter. He was given one key and had another already in his possession. Between them they opened a safe deposit box. Jean-Louis carefully extracted another locked box – this time of wood – then returned the keys. The lift shot him up to his floor and he moved swiftly along the corridor to his room. He let himself in and moved across to the desk. Putting the box down, he found a key in his pocket and unlocked it. He breathed a sigh of contentment then took out the object that lay in the box.

Jean-Louis checked that it was loaded then rammed the clip of bullets back in position. The pistol went into his pocket.

He was ready for the testing time that lay ahead.

The Men's Singles Final produced plenty of entertainment but very little in the way of real drama. There did

215

not seem to be enough at stake for the two players. Each wanted the other to attack and it was only in the third set that real aggression showed. But there were some fine rallies and glorious strokes to applaud. If it was not vintage tennis, it was a very serviceable plonk.

The long interval before the next match gave Hawker the chance to do three important things. He dodged Quentin Rivers – still mourning the dear departed club colleague – and saw Drew Grant taking a seat high in the main stand. Evidently, he had been released by the police and no charges were being pressed. The third matter of importance concerned the mystery over Chegenyov.

It was Christina Erikkson who had the story there. They had a hissed courtside exchange that delivered yet another unexpected development. Christina giggled.

'Yuri has defected.'

'He's what?'

'Seeking asylum in France.'

'You're joking!'

'It's true, Don. Honestly. He went to a police station and begged them to help, apparently. He doesn't want to be Russian any more.'

'Wonderful!'

'I think I may have helped,' said Christina excitedly.

'How?'

'That's the bit I can't work out.'

Yuri Chegenyov was at that moment the subject of high-level discussions in government circles. His defection was seen as a small *coup* for France. She could inflict a pinprick on the Soviet Union and acquire a potential Wimbledon champion at the same time.

Chegenyov himself had no reservations about a decision that had been sitting at the back of his mind for some time. He had no regrets. His country had put

216

him where he was but he had amply repaid her investment. He needed to think for himself now.

France offered him the golden chalice of freedom.

He wanted his own Christina Erikkson.

Well before the Ladies Singles Final got under way, the spectators had threshed themselves into a state of high expectation. Both women had their followings and there was cautious optimism in both camps. Nance Paulson had the greater experience and the better track record in Grand Slam events. Katie Britwell had the stronger motivation and an abiding fondness for slow clay. The recent murder of her husband made for controversy. Would she be able to shrug off her sorrow long enough to give a good account of herself? Would the traumas of the past weeks impinge upon her game. Should she be playing at all so soon after the tragedy?

The talking-points were legion.

When the game started, they became academic. Katie Britwell gained first blood with a break of serve in the fourth game. It was enough to give her a first set that was at once filled with astounding strokeplay and littered with errors from both players.

Hawker studied them at the changeover. Katie was panting, red in the face but quietly thrilled with her advantage. Nance was calm, unruffled and undismayed. She had seen it all before.

The second set was contested even more fiercely. Katie served first. Bouncing the ball four times on the court, she tossed it high then climbed up after it to hit a penetrating serve. The ball bounced right up on the soft clay and Nance hit a short backhand return. Katie's darting speed enabled her to intercept just in front of the service line. She hit a forcing volley that sent Nance deep in the court, well behind the baseline, but the American nevertheless hit a perfect-length return down the line. Katie chased and hit a diagonal backhand that all but beat the outstretched racket of her opponent. A knifing volley came back at her but she sliced it over the net. Nance was there to kill the pace with a delicate drop shot. The gallant Katie made a full-length dive but put the ball into the net.

And so it went on. Total commitment. Aggression. Grace. Speed. Stamina. Style. Sheer character. Rallies lengthened, tension heightened. They were approaching the ethereal standards of their Wimbledon encounter. The crowd was entranced. A single minute could take them through the whole gamut of emotions. Katie improvised superbly and Nance persevered magnificently. Experience had the slight edge and the scores were level.

Katie took her time at the change-over, draping a towel over her head so that she could lose herself in contemplation. She drank half a cup of barley water then came back on court with fresh vigour. It was as if Mel Edmunds was there with her, whispering in her ear every time she played a bad shot, urging her on, helping her out of tight corners, giving her that relentless will to win that had made him invincible in his day. Katie worked for her openings and took them with tigerish relish. She achieved a break of serve and slowly consolidated her advantage.

Nance Paulson looked tired, worried and short of imagination. Her supporters grew silent and her detractors bayed. She was staying in the set but at enormous expense. Katie was goading her to run. Just when it looked as if she was fading, the reigning champion staged one of those remarkable comebacks which made her so difficult to subdue. Winning three games in a row, she got to the brink of victory.

It was Katie's turn to dig deep and find more. Her resilience was equal to the challenge. Finding extra strength and a more lethal accuracy, she pulled back the advantage remorselessly. One rally in the eleventh game lasted over three minutes and involved nearly thirty strokes, each one hit on the sweet spot of the racket to a good length. Katie won the point with a dipping shot that bounced at Nance's feet and left her with no room for manoeuvre.

The match had been decided by that one stroke. It was Katie who forced the pace now and Nance who was thrown on the defensive. With a final flurry that sent the crowd into delirium, the British player clinched the match.

Hawker was as moved as he was delighted. Standing to applaud, he joined the cataract of noise and joy. Katie was ecstatic. Nance was grim and white-faced. Barelli was glowering. Drew Grant was crying. Vincente was planning. Alain Dupont was celebrating. Jean-Louis Croizier was fingering the gun in his pocket. Christina was taking photographs at speed. Dimitri was posing. Daninos and Chabrier were clapping hard.

It had been a far better match than that served up by the men but few of the spectators realized its intrinsic significance. During an hour and a quarter of wondrous tennis, two murders were at last solved. In the bubbling cauldron of the Stade Roland Garros, Hawker found three things that had eluded him for weeks.

Motive. Means. Opportunity.

The presentations were followed by another photographic session then an instant press conference. Katie stayed to celebrate her triumph but the loser slipped quietly away. It was a long time before the cheering died down and the excitement ebbed. As the crowd drifted away, they took with them memories that would return afresh to thrill them. Meanwhile, there were cocktail parties to prolong the adventure of the day and nightime Paris lying ahead with its multiple seductions.

Hawker sparred with Quentin Rivers then stole away to catch Drew Grant. Profoundly moved by Katie's victory, Drew was still close to tears. Hawker asked about his detention.

'I was a marked man, Don,' explained the other. 'I went to Alexander's hotel the night he was killed. I demanded to see him. He wouldn't come out of his room.'

'What did you do?'

'Huffed and puffed and failed to blow the house down.'

'But you upset the management no doubt.'

'They slung me out.'

'I got the same treatment,' said Hawker. 'Those security blokes must've been working overtime.'

Drew's history of confrontations with Robert Alexander had told against him. Having stormed around to the hotel with murderous intent, he had achieved no more than minimal damage to a hotel door. Two days of intensive police questioning had been punishment enough.

'Don't blame the coppers, Drew,' said Hawker.

'Why not?'

'*I* had you pegged as a chief suspect for Mel's murder.'

'Me?'

'There were some photographs of the final in Monte Carlo,' recalled Hawker. 'You were sitting among the spectators.'

Drew Grant laughed then widened his palms to plead.

'All I was doing was watching a tennis match.'

'But you had no reason to be there.'

'I had every reason, old son,' confessed the other. 'Next time you get out those photographs, look at the girl sitting to my left. Carole. She's my assistant at the Kingzett Centre.'

'So what are you telling me?'

'Carole fancied watching some tennis, I fancied a

dirty weekend. So we pushed the boat out and went to Monte Carlo. That way, we both got what we wanted.'

'You weren't there to be near Katie?' said Hawker.

'I had no idea she'd even be there, Don. She was supposed to be playing in the Virginia Slims somewhere in the States. Besides, I had my hands full with Carole. It was nice to see Katie from a distance but she was completely bound up in Mel and had no time for me.'

'Every picture tells a story,' sighed Hawker.

'But not always the right one.'

They shook hands and parted. Hawker went on through to the locker rooms to find that Katie had now departed. The place looked bare and deserted. A few rackets lay about. The tang of disinfectant lingered. This was where the private traumas were endured. The public only saw the battle on the centre court. In the quiet of the locker room, other battles were fought out as players wrestled with their doubts, their limitations and their consciences. Many matches were won and lost before players even got on to the court. Hawker thought of his own dressing room ordeals before big races.

The slam of a door brought him out of his reverie and he saw that yet another battle was to be staged. Vincente was sizing him up and chuckling to himself. Hawker knew he would be back sometime. The bodyguard wanted to change the rules of the contest. Slipping a hand into his pocket, he pulled out a gleaming knuckleduster with a series of sharp spikes on it. When it was fitted on to his right hand, he had a weapon that could rip Hawker apart in seconds. Vincente moved in to demonstrate.

Hawker could not risk a long fight. Escape was the priority. He conceived and executed his plan in a matter of seconds. As the huge Italian lumbered at him, Hawker snatched up a tennis racket and swung it hard. Three shots were all that was needed. Two forehands and a whipped backhand across the face.

Vincente howled in anguish. The gash on his head had been re-opened, his right ear was burning and blood was streaming into his eye from the jagged cut above it. Hawker left him flailing madly and got out.

Nance Paulson was packing her suitcase when she heard the knock on the door. She glanced up at Jean-Louis, shrugged then went through into the other room. Peering through the peep-hole, she saw a far from welcome face. She opened the door to dispatch it.

'Not now, Don. I'm busy.'

'You've got time for me,' he insisted, pushing past her and going into the room. 'Let's talk about Mel Edmunds and Robert Alexander, shall we?'

'Say, what is this?' she demanded.

'The end of the line.'

'You can't just barge in here like this.'

'Would you rather have this chat at the police station?'

'Go screw yourself, buster!'

'Why not close the door?'

Nance glared at him then she pushed the door shut. Walking past him, she gathered up a few books and magazines from the coffee table.

'You'll have to excuse me while I pack,' she said. 'I've got a plane to catch in less than an hour.'

'Not tonight, Nance.'

'Who says so?'

'I do.'

She scooped up three rackets from the sofa and tried to go past him to the bedroom. Hawker stopped her with his enquiry.

'Which one killed Mel? Did you use the same one on Alexander?'

Nance spun round to face him with blazing anger.

'Get out of my hair, mister!'

222

'Want to hear how it was done?' he asked. 'Simple. You invite Mel to a dinner party you *know* is going to be a disaster so that everyone can see what a nasty man he could be. There was no way he and Alain Dupont would hit it off. You deliberately threw them together to get Mel riled up.'

'*I'm* the one who's getting riled up, Don.'

'It was a way of getting back at him for having the temerity to marry Katie. You couldn't bear that, could you? Katie with a man like that. So you went up to the penthouse suite at the Hotel Brassard and you played a little tennis.'

'You got a nerve – I'll say that for you.'

'Mel let you in because you were a friend. Or so he thought. As soon as his back was turned, you hit him with your racket. Then out you went and down the fire escape to the car you had parked directly outside. How far away did you say you lived? Two minutes' drive? That would put you back in your house in less than four minutes from the time you smashed his head in.'

Nance put down what she was holding and squared up to him.

'You forgot to mention *why* I did all this.'

'Katie.'

'That so?'

'You had an affair with her,' he said. 'Robert Alexander found out about it. That's why he was able to blackmail Katie.'

'Alexander was a turd!'

'I'd go along with you there. He knew too much and he had to go. That's the irony of it, Nance. If you'd left him alone, you'd have won that title today.'

'What do you mean?'

'You had a second motive for killing Mel,' he reasoned. 'It wasn't just revenge because he took Katie away from you. He helped her game to improve. She got better while you stayed the same. Katie Britwell was

223

on the way up as you were about to go down.'

'No!' she protested.

'Get rid of Mel and you solve two problems. He's safely out of the way and so is Katie. She was completely broken up by it all and didn't want to play tennis at all. That really suited your book. As it happens, she found her drive again but it was Alexander's death that tipped the balance. Once he was out of the way, the pressures were off. Her game blossomed.'

'You're way out of line, Don.'

'Am I?'

'None of this makes any sense.'

'It does to me, Nance. You signed a confession.'

'I did *what*?'

'Out on that court today,' he explained. 'It's all in the way you play tennis. Neat, ordered, ruthless. You in control. No room for error. When you're on the defensive, you simply hit harder and with more venom. You'd do anything to stay at the top. Even commit murder. Mel was your first victim. A Nance Paulson serve. Deadly.'

'Go on.'

'There was nothing wrong with your elbow when you took a swipe at him, was there? That was another part of your plan. Feign injury to get back to Monte Carlo.'

'It's my home, God dammit!'

'Exactly. Everybody knows you there. You don't stick out because you're one celebrity among a thousand. Nobody would turn a hair if you walked through the lobby of a hotel with a tennis racket. In through the main door. Out through the fire escape. Is that how it was with Alexander as well?'

'You sure been busy figuring all this out, Don.'

'It was worth it.'

'Not quite. You're a little off target.'

'I don't think so.'

'Okay,' she admitted, 'Katie and I had something

going but it only lasted for a couple of weeks. That just wasn't her scene. I talked her into it but she was never comfortable. Katie felt terribly guilty about it. To prove that she wasn't really like that, she picks the most macho guy on the lot.'

'Mel Edmunds.'

'Check.'

'So why am I off target?'

'I didn't hate Mel because of Katie. It was someone else.' She gave a harsh laugh. 'He couldn't wait. Mel didn't even *try* to be faithful to her. He'd only been married a month when he started off again. Only he picked the wrong girl that time.'

Hawker could see a page in an address book. Four names in alphabetical order with Lia Barelli monopolising his attention. He had picked the wrong one as well. He thought of a fresh-faced college girl with pigtails. He thought of a kiss across the net at the Foro Italico. He thought about a doubles victory in the same tournament. He thought of the many photographs in which he had seen them together.

'Jody Beecher!'

'She was mine,' said Nance simply. 'It was beautiful. Just as it should be. Until Mel came along. He shouldn't have touched her. She was all mine.'

The address book again. Jody Beecher's home number in Texas. She was playing on the Virginia Slims Tour in Houston that week. Living at home and available by telephone. Just before he died, Mel was about to call the girl who got him murdered.

'He had a photo of her in his wallet,' recalled Nance. 'I took the wallet and threw it into the sea. I kept the photo.'

Nance was gazing at him with a strange intensity.

'Does your husband know?' he asked.

'Of course, M'sieur.'

Jean-Louis Croizier came in from the bedroom with

225

the gun in his hand. He pointed it at Hawker and offered him a bland smile.

'I know everything now,' said the Frenchman.

'Jean-Louis is a realist,' added his wife. 'Like me. That's why our marriage works so well. He wanted my name. I needed respectability. It's the perfect arrangement.'

'It *was*,' said Hawker. 'Not any more.'

'We will not let you spoil it all, M'sieur,' warned Jean-Louis.

'You know too much, Don.'

'Like Robert Alexander.'

'Yes,' she said. 'He went too far. That's why he had to be taken out of the game. Alexander was very clever. Although his main interest was in Katie, he kept tabs on me as well. He found out about Jody and he tried to use that information against me.'

'Blackmail?'

'Not for money.'

'Then what?'

'Something far more precious. My professional pride.'

'I don't follow.'

'Alexander was crazy about Katie. He'd do anything and everything to help her. His dream was to make her the number one on the woman's tour. Then, of course, he'd marry her and they'd live happily ever after.' Nance curled her lip in a sneer. 'Only I happened to be in the way. So he told me to do the one thing I couldn't.'

'Lose the final to Katie.'

'Yes. Making sure that she herself never suspected it. Hell! I've never thrown a match in my life and I never will. Nobody can make me do that.' The irony amused her. 'Funny thing is, Katie didn't need any help from me. Beat me fair and square.'

'Only after you'd eliminated Alexander.'

'It was necessary,' said Jean-Louis. 'I'm afraid that Monsieur Alexander was too inquisitive. He began prying into the affairs of Bellecroix. He objected to certain practices that we use. Business is a jungle. We have to survive.'

'Get the picture?' asked Nance.

'Alexander was hustling the both of you.'

'He had to go,' said Jean-Louis.

'Just like you, Don.'

'Now, wait a minute,' advised Hawker. 'You don't think I'd be stupid enough to come here on my own, do you?'

'Finish him off,' urged Nance.

'I rang the police,' he said. 'They'll be here any minute.'

'He's bluffing, Jean-Louis.'

'The odds are stacked against you this time, Nance.'

She was his only hope. Jean-Louis was standing some yards away with the revolver at the ready. Nance was still within reach. He tried to detain her for a few vital seconds.

'Just tell me one thing,' he asked.

'Time's up, Don.'

'How come *your* name was in Mel's address book?'

'What?'

'He had a Boston phone number for you. I thought . . .'

'Don't insult me!' she snarled. 'I wasn't one of his girls. He had my number because we used to play doubles at one time, that's all.'

It was enough. Hawker made a sudden dive for Nance and used her as a shield. As Jean-Louis tried to aim the gun, Hawker hurled his wife at him. In the confusion, he lunged forward and grabbed the Frenchman's wrist. There was a fierce struggle. Nance pounded on Hawker's back with her fists then rushed to grab a tennis racket. Slipping it out of its cover, she

227

raised it high to deliver a killer blow. But she was stopped in her tracks. As Hawker twisted Jean-Louis's wrist, the gun went off and the bullet went straight through Nance's forearm. She dropped the racket with a scream of pain. Her husband was distracted for a second and Hawker took full advantage, seizing the gun from him and clubbing him to the carpet.

He was still standing over them when the police arrived.

Inspector Fournier and his *agents* took over. Hawker surrendered the gun. A tide of relief washed over him. Nance was kneeling on the floor, clutching at her arm and sobbing quietly. Jean-Louis was tending her. Hawker felt no sympathy for either of them just a deep satisfaction that it was all over and that he had fulfilled his promise to Katie Britwell. It had taken time but he had found Mel's killer.

Chief Inspector Yves Daninos and Sergeant Raoul Chabrier walked in on the tableau. Daninos was impressed but Chabrier was peeved that he had missed out on the action.

Hawker beckoned them across.

'You were right.'

'Was I?' said Daninos.

'*Crime passionnel.*'

'That is as it should be, M'sieur.'

Christina Erikkson woke in an empty bed and sighed her disappointment. It had been their last night together. They had reached the parting of the ways. She had hoped in vain for a proper farewell.

Somewhere out in the rainswept streets of Paris, a bulky figure was pounding his way along the pavements. He ignored the splash of water on his legs. He did not feel the increased force of the downpour. The soaking vest and shorts did not bother him. The sodden hair was only a minor discomfort.

Don Hawker moved on with the relentless stride of a man who must keep on running towards an unknown destination. It was a journey that he had to make on his own.

SKINWALKERS

Tony Hillerman

Three unexpected and apparently unconnected murders
on the Big Reservation lead to whispers of witchcraft –
which Lt. Joe Leaphorn, determinedly rational, does not
believe in. But then there are the bone heads . . .
Reluctantly, Leaphorn enlists Officer Jim Chee, with his
knowledge of Navajo lore – only to find that Chee himself
is somehow involved in a tangle of dark mysticism and
more complex, modern evil that threatens them both . . .

Also by Tony Hillerman in Sphere Books:

THE GHOSTWAY
THE DARK WIND
PEOPLE OF DARKNESS
A THIEF OF TIME
TALKING GOD

0 7474 0231 X
CRIME

THE ANDERSON TAPES

Lawrence Sanders

It was a brilliant scheme, a heist that couldn't fail. The one that would get him out at last. All it needed was careful planning – and Anderson always planned carefully.

But Anderson doesn't know he's got more electronic listeners than he's got team members. The CIA are bugging his money men. Narcotics have a tap on his kinky mistress. THE NYPD monitor all his own calls. The IRS, the FBI, and the US Secret Service are all in the audience too.

If the listeners ever got together, they'd have Anderson taped . . .

0 7474 0460 7
THRILLER

Sphere now offers an exciting range of quality fiction and non-fiction by both established and new authors. All of the books in this series are available from good bookshops, or can be ordered from the following address:

Sphere Books
Cash Sales Department
P.O. Box 11
Falmouth
Cornwall TR10 9EN.

Please send cheque or postal order (no currency), and allow 60p for postage and packing for the first book plus 25p for the second book and 15p for each additional book ordered up to a maximum charge of £1.90 in U.K.

B.F.P.O. customers please allow 60p for the first book, 25p for the second book plus 15p per copy for the next 7 books, thereafter 9p per book.

Overseas customers including Eire please allow £1.25 for postage and packing for the first book, 75p for the second book and 28p for each subsequent title ordered.